Fifteen Hands

Jane Sorenson

STANDARD PUBLISHING
Cincinnati, Ohio   2983

Library of Congress Cataloging in Publication Data

Sorenson, Jane
  Fifteen hands.

  (A Jennifer book ; 7)
  Summary: Jennifer's excitement over the Winter
Carnival and her new horse is tempered by her friend
Chris' problems with her alcoholic mother.
  [1. Friendship—Fiction. 2. Christian life—
Fiction. 3. Alcoholism—Fiction] I. Title.
II. Series: Sorenson, Jane. Jennifer book ; 7.
PZ7.S7214Fi 1985   [Fic]   85-2594
ISBN 0-87239-933-8

To my niece
Becky McDonald Goddard,
who owned and loved the real Snap.
And to
Wayne "Butch" Goddard
who loves Becky.

Chapter 1

Heidi's Secret

Lord, it's me, Jennifer.

Until lately, I always zonked out the minute my head hit the pillow. So, as You know, lying here awake is really weird. This is the second time in a week that I've been too excited to sleep.

My first time involved two of the Harrington brothers, Matthew and Mack. Here, in Philadelphia, junior high includes grades seven, eight, and nine. Matthew's in ninth. Mack and I are in eighth. The problem was I liked both of them and that's why I couldn't sleep!

As my grandma told me, You do have a way of working things out. Naturally, we're all too young to make permanent choices! But what happened was that Matthew asked me to go to the big basketball game. And Mack asked my friend Heidi. Then the four of us all went together. Personally, I think it was the highlight of my life! Well, at least one of them.

But that was *last week!* Are You still with me? You know, one of the nicest things about telling You everything is that You hang in there!

The big deal this Saturday is the Winter Carnival. Because I'm the newest kid in school, naturally I couldn't run for "queen." But I picked up a petition for Heidi. Since I hadn't told her about it, she was really surprised this morning to see her name on the ballot!

Lying here now, I still can't get it through my head that she really won! A teacher called her tonight to tell her. That's so she can be prepared with a white queen dress Saturday night.

Don't tell anyone! It's a secret! I'm not even supposed to know. But naturally, Heidi called me. And she said I could call Grandma Green in Florida. But no one else can know. Even Heidi doesn't know who got it for "king"! I suppose You do. Right? But don't tell me. I want to be surprised!

Lord, thanks for making my life so interesting! Maybe what happens to me doesn't seem like a big deal to You, but I think it's better than TV. What happens next in my life is so *personal,* You know.

*   *   *   *   *

"Couldn't you sleep?" Mom asked.

"What makes you think that?" I casually reached for my orange juice and sipped it slowly. You can only act cool when you have plenty of time.

"That was your door I heard opening last night, wasn't it?"

"Can't a person have any privacy?" I asked. I got a shell in my soft-boiled egg. I spent so much time being cool that I had to hurry to make the bus.

"You don't have to tell me about the phone call," Mom said. She smiled.

"Thanks." I smiled back. "By the way, I won't be home after school. Heidi and I have something to do. But if anyone calls, don't tell where I am or who I'm with."

"*That* secret?"

"Heavy duty," I told her. "You'll know soon."

"I can hardly wait," Mom said, smiling. It sounded kind of like a put-down, but I ignored it.

On my way to the bus stop, I decided I'd better sober up. Although I'm pretty cool, I'm not excellent at hiding my emotions. As You've probably noticed.

I mean, even when I was little, everyone knew when I had the Old Maid. And Chris McKenna, my riding-teacher-friend, recently guessed I had a boyfriend when all I did was order a Western-burger at Reuben's!

Being cool in front of Stephanie and Lindsay was no problem. They didn't even look at me. Probably they were surprised to see Heidi's name on the ballot too! I wonder how they'll act when they hear she won!

7

The girls didn't even look up when the Harrington brothers arrived. Which is unusual.

"Looks like we picked the right date for the Winter Carnival," Matthew grinned.

"What do you mean?" I asked.

"I guess you didn't hear about the snow," Mack said.

"I guess I didn't. What snow?"

"It's supposed to snow tonight. Hope your mom has plenty of groceries on hand," Matthew said.

"You forget that we lived in Chicago," I said. "What's the big deal?"

They glanced at each other. "I just hope the Winter Carnival isn't canceled," Matthew said.

"You've got to be kidding!" I said. But I could tell that they weren't.

We took our usual seats on the bus. I saved the one next to me for Heidi. Stephanie and Lindsay sat behind me and whispered. I ignored them.

I remembered back to the start of school. Back when Heidi's warm smile meant so much. We had met in Sunday school. And, although she wasn't cool, she was the only girl from my class attending my school.

I watched her get on. Now she wears contacts, and her hair is styled, and her clothes are sharp. But, somehow, *cool* doesn't describe her. Maybe because the first thing you notice is still her warm smile.

"Hi, Jennifer," she grinned.

"Hi," I grinned back. "How're you doing?"

"Cinderella!" she whispered.

I realized that we had to get our act together and stop grinning at each other, or everyone would guess, for sure. "What's planned for this afternoon?"

Heidi talked softly. "Mom's picking us up at the main entrance right after school."

"Are there stores nearby where we can look for the pattern and material?" I talked softly too.

"Right," she said. "No problem."

"Did you bring your color book?" I asked.

"Oh, no! I forgot! I'll call Mom and have her bring it."

"Good," I said. We both used to think that all whites were the same. But that was before we *had our colors done*. We both happen to look best in "soft white," not "pure white."

"Have you heard about the snow?" she asked.

I couldn't believe it. "Why is everyone so paranoid about snow?" I asked. "I never heard so much worry about it in my whole life."

"You mean everything didn't stop when it snowed in Chicago?"

"Of course not," I said. "Well, once we had such a bad storm that we got out of school for two days."

"How did people get around?"

"How else?" I answered. "They drove."

"It's different here," Heidi said.

"That's what Matthew told me. But I don't get it."

"People stay home. School is called off."

"Well, I don't think my family will be scared to drive," I said. "We're used to it."

The day was a pretty normal one. Except that Mack was hyper. "I really think Heidi has a chance to win," he said in homeroom. He sits behind me.

I put on my cool-but-interested look and turned around. "What makes you think so?"

"A lot of the guys on the basketball team were talking in the locker room. With three ninth-grade girls on the ballot, the vote is pretty much split. And lots of kids think Heidi's nice," Mack said.

"I hope she does win," I said. I turned around before he could see my give-away grin. Half the fun will be surprising everyone!

* * * * *

I really didn't know Mrs. Stoltzfus at all. But I figured Heidi's mom would be plump and plain. She is neither. So much for stereotypes!

"You must be Jennifer Green." She has the same friendly smile as Heidi.

"Hi," I said, as I climbed into the car next to Heidi. "I haven't seen you around church, have I?"

She smiled some more. Not laughed. Smiled. "I teach the four year olds," she said. "And I'm in charge of the nursery."

"You must like little kids," I said. It sounded kind of dumb.

"I love little kids," Mrs. Stoltzfus said. "So does Jesus."

10

"Mom's really special with them," Heidi said. "She's one of those people who has a gift for working with kids."

"I wish you had been my teacher when I was little," I said. She had pulled out into the traffic. "I didn't go to Sunday school at all until seventh grade."

"How did that happen?" she asked.

"Well," I said, "it's kind of a long story." The way I tell things, it would take until past midnight!

"You'll have to come over for dinner sometime and tell us all about it," she said.

"I guess you must be proud to have your daughter be Winter Carnival queen," I said, glancing at Heidi.

"Heidi is a beautiful person," her mother said. "I've always seen that part of her."

"Mom!" Heidi said.

"It's true," I agreed. I didn't want anyone to know that I used to think Heidi was out of it.

"Of course, I'm learning some things about clothes myself," Heidi's mom said. "My own childhood was very different from that of our neighbors."

I didn't know what to say. Luckily, we were turning into a shopping center. There, in the middle, was a fabric store.

When I admitted I had never done any real sewing, Mrs. Stoltzfus told me we'd check out the fabric possibilities first. We carried around Heidi's little book of colored fabric swatches.

"This is the right color," Heidi said.

"But doesn't it look like a wedding dress?" Mrs. Stoltzfus wondered. "How about this?"

Frankly, I couldn't picture any of them made into a dress! Fortunately, Heidi and her mother narrowed down the possibilities to three, and we headed for the pattern books.

This wasn't much easier. Many of the styles were obviously too mature for an eighth grader. Others were too fancy. Some looked like Halloween costumes.

"If we did this one in the voile, we could cut it off next summer," Mrs. Stoltzfus suggested.

"Right," said Heidi. "What do you think, Jennifer?"

"You mean it would be regular length?" I asked.

"I could wear it for church or parties," she said. "How often would I wear a long, white dress?"

I could see the point. "You could run for Winter Carnival queen again," I suggested. "Or you could save it in case I got lucky!"

Even Heidi's mother laughed. She asked the salesperson for the pattern in Heidi's size. And they carried over two bolts of fabric, one for the dress and another for a slip. They quickly assembled thread, buttons, zipper, and something called facing.

While the fabric was being measured, Mrs. Stoltzfus glanced at her watch. "I'd better stop at the market on the way home," she said. "They're predicting snow for tonight."

The parking lot at the grocery store was crowded. So far, not a single flake had fallen. I couldn't believe it.

Chapter 2

More Good News

Lord, it's me, Jennifer.

It was dark when Heidi and her mom dropped me off at home. Because we have timers to turn our lights on, it's hard to tell who's home and what's going on.

"Hi, Jennifer," Pete said. My sixth-grade brother was sitting in the living room. Hardly anybody sits in there, especially before dinner.

"Hi! What're you doing?" It was a relief to be able to smile without worrying that I'd give away the secret.

"I'm thinking," Pete said. "What are you grinning about?"

"Was I grinning?" I stuck my books on the stairs and hung up my coat. "Where's everybody?"

"Justin's at basketball practice. And Mom went to get groceries. She said it's going to snow."

"I can't believe it," I said. "Why, all of a sudden, is snow such a big deal?" I sat on the love seat.

"I asked Mike. He said they aren't used to it here," my brother told me. "See, in Chicago we had whole fleets of plows and sand trucks and salt spreaders."

"Don't they have them here?"

"Not many. They don't use salt at all. And people are afraid to drive."

"How about school?" I wondered.

"We'll have to listen to the radio. Each school has a number. They read off the numbers of the ones that are closed."

The garage door opener announced Mom's arrival. "I'll help her carry stuff in," Pete said. I nearly fainted.

At dinner, Dad told us that even an inch of snow causes problems in some cities. "Not every city has public transportation. You know—commuter trains or subways or elevated trains," he said. "In Washington, DC they close government offices in the middle of the afternoon so people can drive home."

"I think I'm going to enjoy the winters here," said Justin.

"Maybe we can make some money shoveling," Pete said.

"Not until *our* lane is done," Dad said.

"By the way," Mom told me, "Chris called this afternoon while you were gone. She wants you to call her."

14

After dinner, I was on pots and pans. Sometimes it seems like I'm always on pots and pans. When I have my own apartment, I'm going to cook everything in the microwave. On paper towels. Unfortunately, microwave ovens aren't so terrific for larger families.

The phone rang before I was done. As usual, it was for me. I left the skillet in the sink and dried my hands. "This is Jennifer Green," I said.

It was Matthew. "Missed you on the bus this afternoon," he said. "Dentist?"

"Not really," I said.

"Twin Pines stables?" he guessed.

"I'll tell you in a couple of days," I said. "I promise."

"Junior-high basketball practice?"

"You can check that out with Mack," I reminded him. "I said I'll tell you later."

"Hey, Jennifer," he said softly. "Don't be mad. I was just curious. Forgive me?"

"Sure," I said. "Hey, I've got a question. What happens if we can't have the Winter Carnival?"

"You mean if we're snowed out? I'm not sure," he said. "I don't think it's ever happened."

"I've never lived in a place where things have been called off."

"It may just be a false alarm," Matthew admitted. "Sometimes people overreact."

"Isn't the committee supposed to put up the decorations tomorrow night?" I asked him.

"Right! We'll pick you up at seven. OK?"

"I'm getting excited," I admitted.

"Me too!" he said. "See you in the morning!"

I resumed my position in front of the sink. Well, Lord, getting back to the skillet after talking on the phone to Matthew was the pits. I couldn't decide whether to change to hot water or try to finish with what was already there.

No decision, because the phone rang again. Naturally, it was for me!

"It's Chris," she said. She sounded excited, which for her is unusual.

"I was going to call you as soon as I got done in the kitchen," I explained. "What's up?"

"Remember a girl at Twin Pines named Emily?" Chris asked.

I remembered. She occasionally had lessons before me last summer. And she was the most unfriendly person I've ever met. Much worse than Stephanie and Lindsay.

"She quit coming months ago," Chris said. "Today I heard that her horse, Snap, is for sale. I think he might be a good one for you to consider!"

"I can't believe it!" I said. "Can you find out more about him for my dad?"

"I had that in mind," Chris said. "But I thought you might like to look him over. Can you come tomorrow afternoon?"

"Can I!" I said. "Just a sec, I'll check with Mom."

"It's Chris," I told my parents. "She says there's a horse for sale at Twin Pines. Can either of you take me

16

over tomorrow after school to see him?"

Mom agreed. I ran back to the phone. "All set," I told her. "See you right after school! Hey, Chris, I'm hyper!"

"I told you if Ashlie's horse didn't work out, there'd be another one!"

"And I believed you," I told her. "But I didn't expect it to happen so soon! Thanks, Chris!"

I rushed into the family room, where my parents were reading. They were expecting me. Dad had already folded up the newspaper.

"Snap's been boarded at Twin Pines as long as I've been taking lessons there," I told Dad. "His owner is a girl named Emily. Chris was starting to teach her to jump last summer."

As You know, my parents are open to the idea of my getting a horse. I've been taking lessons from Chris since we moved to Philadelphia.

Recently, we came close to buying a different horse, but it turned out to have problems. "I hope it works out this time, Jennifer," Dad said, smiling. "You certainly acted mature when you were disappointed."

"Thanks," I said modestly. Then I let out a shriek that was anything but mature. It brought Justin running from the basement!

Well, by the time I returned to the skillet, I had no choice. I had to let out the cold water and start over. But somehow I didn't even mind.

Chapter 3

Snowed In

Lord, it's me, Jennifer.

I can't believe it. Now I can't get to sleep because of the horse!

As You know, I've wanted a horse forever! Well, You know what I mean. It seems that long. But now that it seems to be happening, I'm afraid to get my hopes up! It's like if I get too enthused, it will fall through again. Know what I mean?

Last Christmas I was so sure I was getting a horse. In my head I was riding off into the sunset. Which was kind of stupid, since I had never even touched a horse. As You know.

I can still remember how I felt when Dad told me I was

getting a new bedroom set instead! Like laughing and crying all at the same time. Laughing where it showed. Crying where it didn't.

Well, getting to take riding lessons was a super part of our move here from Illinois. I mean, now I have actual experience. Chris even thinks I'm pretty good at it.

And I sure lucked out getting Chris for a teacher. By the way, did You pick her out?

I guess she was my first girl friend in Pennsylvania. After all, we are the same age. Naturally, our families are very different. But when she came for dinner that first time, she was the first girl I could really talk to. And we've been honest with each other ever since.

Frankly, I was counting on getting Ashlie's horse. Did You realize that? I even had it all figured out that You had planned it. Well, wrong-o!

So now part of me is super excited. But there's a little voice in my head that says, "Don't count on it. Then it won't hurt so much if it doesn't work out!"

Please, Lord, can You handle this? I really do need my sleep.

P. S. Amen.

* * * * *

When I woke up, I heard scraping outside. I peeked out one of my front windows. Everything was white. Except someone who was shoveling his heart out. Usually I get dressed right away, but when I went to the bath-

20

room, I could see Justin's door open. And people were talking downstairs. I grabbed my warm robe and slipper-socks.

"Hi, Pete," I said, since he was the only person in sight. "What's happening?"

"The snow is really deep," he said. "Justin's listening to the radio to see if school's called off. I'm going out to help Dad shovel as soon as I eat."

"Where's Mom?"

"She got all bundled up and went outside. Something to do with feeding the birds! If you can believe that!"

I could.

"Yahoo!" Justin yelled. "No school! Pete, they just called our number!"

I hurried down to the family room. "How do you know that's your school?" I asked. "Don't they give names?"

"Nope," he said. "Just numbers. It's like a secret code. Or a lottery."

I listened. He was right. "In Delaware County, 17, 39, 200. Keep tuned for more school closings after this message."

"Did you hear my school?" I asked.

"What's the number?"

"I don't know," I admitted.

"You've got to be kidding!"

"How did you find out your number?" I was feeling desperate.

"I can't remember. I think it was on a paper they sent

21

home. I don't know." I turned and looked out the big window overlooking the back of the house. The tree looked *flocked*. You know, with snow stuck onto all the branches. And it was full of birds. Just sitting there.

The feeder was also covered with snow. And the weight of the snow had closed off the supply of sunflower seeds.

Mom waved as she came around the corner of the porch. Which wasn't easy. The snow was above her boots, and she had to lift her feet high. Her hair was stuck under a rust-colored knit cap, and she carried a broom. She looked like someone—or something—left over from Halloween.

Some of the birds flew away as she neared the feeder. But many stayed and watched her sweep off the "front porch" of the feeder. Immediately, the bird station was open for business.

Mom looked at me and smiled. She stepped back and watched a chickadee come in for a landing. I smiled too. She turned to come back in.

What worried me was not knowing about school. I had no idea where to look for that number. Which meant that I would have to call somebody. I felt really stupid. Like really dumb.

Justin was pouring a bowl of cereal, and Pete was putting on his down coat and boots. "I'm going out to help Dad," he said. "Are you guys coming?"

"As soon as I eat," Justin said. "Do we have enough shovels?"

"We'll soon find out," Pete said.

22

I jumped when the phone rang. "Green residence," I said. "Jennifer Green speaking."

"*Now* do you believe it?" It was Matthew. He was laughing.

"Believe what?" I teased.

"No way a school bus could navigate these hills today!"

"School's called off, I take it?"

"Didn't you know?" he asked.

"Not until now," I said. "What about the Winter Carnival?"

"A lot can happen by tomorrow night," Matthew said. "We may even be able to get out by this afternoon. I'll let you know later, after I talk to Megan."

"Right," I said. "Bye."

Mom was warming up with a cup of coffee. "Isn't this beautiful?" she beamed.

"Shall I eat first or get dressed?" I asked.

She didn't answer.

"I'll just be a minute," I said. I rushed upstairs and put on jeans, warm socks, a couple of layers of sweater stuff. And moisturizer. I just read that I should begin now to keep my skin nice. In fact, I should have started long ago. I hate being behind.

Honestly, I just took a few minutes, but no one was left in the kitchen. As I drank my orange juice, I could hear the radio still droning school closing numbers.

By the time I had some cereal and a piece of raisin toast, I could hear Dad stomping his feet in the entry. "I

23

never realized how long that lane was," he complained. "I think if we get the turn-around cleared, I can get a fast start up the hill and make it."

"Can't get out?" Mom asked. She was in the family room watching a squirrel's unsuccessful attempt to raid the bird feeder.

"Are you kidding?" he said. "I might as well join you for a minute while I catch my breath." He came into the kitchen and poured himself a cup of coffee.

"Hi," I said. "Are we snowed in?"

"Of course not," he answered. "Want to take a turn helping? My shovel is free."

"Sure," I said. "I'll get my jacket and boots."

I won't say it looked hopeless. But the area near the basketball pole wasn't even finished, and Pete and Justin were puffing away. "What should I do?" I asked.

"Beats me," said Pete. "I guess you could try over there. Dad wants to gun it out to the road."

I started working.

"We could build a fort," Justin said.

"Gotta get Dad out first," Pete said.

Pretty soon I was puffing too. The snow was heavy.

Just as Dad came back out, so did the sun. Come out, I mean. The glare was almost blinding.

Pete handed Dad his shovel. "I'm pooped," he said.

Dad surveyed the progress. "I think I'll try to get the car out."

"You'll never make it," Justin said.

"Thanks," said Dad.

24

Well, he didn't. On the second try, his back wheels got stuck in the turn-around. Everybody pushed. On the ninth try, he made it about halfway up the lane. But that was it.

"I'll have to call the office," he said. "I can't believe it."

Chapter 4

Snap Judgment

Lord, it's me, Jennifer.

By the middle of the morning, it was clear that Dad wasn't too thrilled with Your surprise snow day.

"Relax," Mom told him. "Enjoy the beauty!"

"That's easy for you to say," my father said. "You aren't giving a presentation Monday morning!"

"True," Mom said. Dad disappeared into the study.

"I've never seen anything so beautiful in my life," Mom said. "Look at those birds!"

Well, I agreed. The sight of the red cardinals decorating that white tree was spectacular. Because the feeder was so popular, lots of birds had to wait their turn. If too many got on the porch at one time, their weight closed off the food. They caught on pretty fast, in my opinion.

Pete and Justin got permission to go down to the Harringtons, where the action was. I'm not sure what action, but I'm sure it involved the snow.

The doorbell rang. I jumped. Our doorbell hardly ever rings. "Want your lane plowed?" a guy said.

"Just a second," I told him. "I'll check."

Dad went for it. I watched out the window while the small tractor cleared the snow into huge banks along the side. Having the car stuck in the middle was a problem solved by hand shoveling. Dad helped.

"All set," Dad said, briefcase in hand. But he stormed back in a few minutes later.

"What's wrong?" Mom asked.

"I'll tell you what's wrong," Dad shouted. "The road isn't plowed! That's what's wrong!"

Well, I guess Mom didn't know what to say, because she didn't say anything. Pretty soon he went back into his study.

"Why are those birds down on the ground?" I asked.

"I can't figure it out either. They seem to be eating the shells and whatever falls down from the other birds," Mom said. She took out her bird book. "I guess they're sparrows."

Personally, I couldn't settle down to do anything. Maybe I'm more like Dad. Do You think so?

I called Heidi for a report on her dress.

"It's going to be beautiful, Jennifer," she said. "Speaking of Cinderella!"

"Can you tell what it will look like already?"

"Mom cut it out last night, and I've already had two fittings," she reported. "I wonder if I'll have a crown?"

"You should," I said. "Queens always have crowns."

"But can you imagine one of those guys wearing a crown?" Heidi started laughing.

I laughed too. It was pretty funny. "I wonder who it'll be? You know, I think Matthew and Mack are going to flip out when they see you!"

"So will some of the other kids!" Heidi said.

I had to agree. Although Heidi is really nice, she hadn't always been popular because kids thought she wasn't cool.

Well, we just kept talking. I didn't realize for how long until my father came and pointed at his watch. I hung up without our discussing the possibility of the Winter Carnival being postponed. That couldn't happen. No way.

I decided to read. I have a book report due next week anyway, but somehow I found it hard to concentrate.

"Telephone," Mom called. "Jennifer!"

"This is Jennifer Green," I said. Very cool.

"Hi! It's Chris. What are you doing?"

"Nothing special," I admitted. "How about you?" For sure she wasn't in school either.

"Can you go to Twin Pines after lunch?" she asked. "About one o'clock?"

"We're snowed in," I said. "Our road hasn't been plowed."

"Felix will take us in the four-wheel-drive jeep."

29

"Can he make it in deep snow?" I wondered.

"Probably. But just in case, can you walk down to the highway? We can pick you up at the corner."

I checked with Mom. "I'll be there," I said. "Will we be riding the horses?"

"Let's take our pants and boots in case we want to. Mainly I'm sure you want to look at Snap."

"How'd you guess?" I laughed. The excitement all came back! As You probably noticed.

By a quarter to one, my brothers were eating at Harringtons, Dad was climbing the walls, and Mom had spotted a red-bellied woodpecker. With my riding boots and pants in my tote bag, I left the house.

It is about half a mile to the "highway." I'm not sure why they call it that, unless it's because it has a route number. Frankly, we had side streets in Illinois that got more traffic!

The walk was beautiful. Naturally, it's the first time I've seen snow here. It seemed whiter, which sounds kind of dumb. Maybe it's just that it hadn't been plowed. Anyhow, the sky was so blue, and the sunshine made everything sparkle. Your Winter Carnival! Right?

Suddenly, I realized how quiet it was. You know what? There weren't any people! No kids throwing snowballs or neighbors hollering to each other while they shoveled. Was *everybody* at Harringtons?

I stood on the corner. At first I didn't recognize them. Of course, a jeep looks pretty different from a limo. But as Felix slowed down, I nearly laughed out loud. Instead of his chauffeur's uniform, he wore a red plaid jacket and a red knit cap!

"Hi, Jennifer!" Chris looked really happy. No solemn riding instructor. No cool kid. No red eyes.

I climbed in beside her. Then I yelled "Yahoo!" So much for not getting my hopes up!

I could see Felix smiling. "Chris tells me there's a horse for sale," he said.

"But she could care less," Chris teased.

I laughed. "Do you ride?" I asked Felix.

"I've done some in my day," he said. When he turned off the highway, he had no trouble with the snow. I couldn't believe all the cars and trucks and jeeps parked at Twin Pines. "Looks like everybody has the same idea," he said.

"Give us a couple of hours," Chris told him. "I told Dad and Mom I'd be back before four."

I glanced at her. I think it's the first time I've ever heard her mention her parents both at the same time. Usually she talks about her Mom's drinking or her father's working. Is that why she's so happy today? Just wondered, You know.

We headed straight for Snap's stall. We stopped and looked in.

Suddenly, it was like I was the only one in the whole stable. Snap certainly was expecting me. He looked up and walked slowly toward me. I took a step closer. Fumbling in my pocket, I came up with the carrot I had taken from the refrigerator. I put it in the feed trough. He ate it.

Then he reached his head toward me. I touched his nose. Time stopped.

"You are beautiful," I told him. "Probably you are the most beautiful horse in the whole world." I kept patting him. Obviously, he believed me.

Finally, Chris broke the magic moment. "Well, what do you think?"

I just stood there grinning.

"See," she teased, "I knew you'd get emotional!"

"Do you believe in love at first sight?" I asked. "You do think he loves me, don't you?"

"It looks pretty mutual!" She grinned too. Then she reached over and gave Snap a pat too.

"There's nothing wrong with him, is there?" I had to know.

"No. That's one reason I wanted you to see him. He's been checked out by the vet. And the price is fair for a horse of his quality. But there's no point in telling your dad about him if *you* don't want him."

"Would you believe I've never been so enthused in my whole life?" I asked.

"Yes, I'd believe it." She kept looking at me and smiling. "And I'll bet when you were a child, everyone always knew when you had the Old Maid!" she said.

"I can't believe it," I said. "How did you know?"

Chapter 5

All Systems Are "Go"

Lord, it's me, Jennifer.

It wasn't that I didn't enjoy riding Rocky. He is like an old friend, and I'm very loyal to my old friends. But, to be honest, all I could think of the whole time was Snap!

"Is there a *catch*, Chris?" I asked. She watched as I groomed Rocky. "If Snap is so good, why is Emily selling him?"

"You might find this hard to believe, but she never really wanted to ride in the first place!" Chris told me.

Chris was right. I did find it hard to believe. "Why wouldn't she? I thought nearly every girl went through a phase of wanting her own horse."

"It wasn't Emily's idea," Chris said. "Her parents

belong to the Hunt Club. They bought Snap and set up lessons because they know my parents and me."

"Like being forced to take piano lessons because your mother is a piano teacher?"

"You've got it," Chris said. "It became sort of a power struggle. And Emily won."

"Maybe she lost," I said.

"Maybe."

"Didn't your mother put you on a horse before you could walk?" I asked. "How come you didn't rebel?"

"I did," Chris said.

"I don't get it."

"Have you ever wondered why a kid like me gives lessons and cleans my own stable? Or why my horse is at Twin Pines instead of on our family property?" Chris asked.

"You mean you have horses at home?"

"Sure. Didn't you notice our stables?"

"I didn't," I admitted. Of course, I was only there once. And I was so blown away by the mansion and the servants and Mrs. McKenna, I couldn't observe *everything!*

"Well, now you know."

"Chris, I'm so glad you were here to give me lessons and be my friend!" I said.

"Me too. I just hate it when kids learn bad habits. And it will be fun for me having you here, I must admit!" Chris smiled.

"Be honest," I said. "Weren't you afraid if I got

Ashlie's horse I'd ride with Lindsay and Stephanie?"

"Sure," she admitted. "But I didn't overprice him. The Cantrells took care of that themselves."

We timed it just about right. Felix was waiting when we came out.

"Look! The road's been plowed," I noticed. But when we got to my house, there was Dad with a shovel!

"What happened?" I asked.

"Now I can't get out because they left this pile of snow in front of the lane," he said. He stood up. "Hi, Chris! And you must be Felix."

"Yes, Sir." He was very respectful. I hoped Dad wouldn't ask him to shovel! He didn't.

"Well, Chris, does this horse still look good?"

"It does, Mr. Green. I couldn't recommend Snap for everyone, but I'm sure Jennifer can handle him. Do you want to take a look?" Chris asked.

"I probably should," Dad said. "Not that I'd know what to look for anyway." He looked at Felix. "Sort of like kicking the tires on a new car," he said.

"Tomorrow morning about ten?" Chris suggested. "I think you ought to get an offer in as soon as possible."

"We'll meet you there," Dad said. "OK, Jennifer?"

I grinned as I climbed out of the jeep. Naturally, it's OK!

Mom could tell the minute I got into the house that I was excited. "He's beautiful!" I kept saying. "Brown with white on his forehead. And," I added, "he's fifteen hands high."

"You can explain that later, Jennifer. Matthew Harrington has been trying all afternoon to reach you," Mom said. "I told him you'd call as soon as you got home."

"This is Jennifer Green," I said. "May I please speak to Matthew?"

"Hi, Jennifer," he said. "All systems are 'go' for the Winter Carnival! Everyone's going to be putting up booths and decorations at the gym tonight."

"I am *so* glad," I said.

"Mark's driving the station wagon over. Can we pick you up about seven-thirty?"

"Terrific," I said. Mom was gesturing. "Just a minute."

"Please ask him to send your brothers home," she whispered.

"Mom wants you to tell Pete and Justin to come home, OK?"

"Right. See you tonight! Bye."

I hung up and stood there a minute. Lord, I think I'm the happiest girl in the world. Hey, thanks!

* * * * *

After I showered, I put on clean jeans and a pale blue shirt and my Nikes. And moisturizer.

Matthew rang our doorbell just like he does when he takes me out. Well, we've gone somewhere together twice. But every time counts, doesn't it? Lord, is decorating the gym a date?

36

Well, romantic it was not! Mark Harrington, who drove, is a high-school senior. He told jokes that were worse than Justin's. And, of course, we had to pick up Megan. And Oswald.

Oswald, You'll recall, is the name we gave to the huge styrofoam snowman our committee made. He goes on the platform where the king and queen will be presented. It took both Matthew and his brother to get Oswald out of the house without breaking him.

And Megan, You'll recall, is the ninth-grade girl who's trying to catch Matthew. Only he doesn't know it. I keep forgetting how pretty she is until I see her again! Tonight she wore tight jeans. My father wouldn't even let me out the front door in jeans that tight! Frankly, I don't know how she expected to help much.

"Were you surprised today by the snow?" Megan asked Matthew.

He was trying to maneuver Oswald through a glass double-door without breaking the styrofoam head off. Clearly, she hasn't spent much time helping her father on projects at home or she wouldn't have tried to start a conversation at such a moment!

Matthew made a disgusted sound exactly like Dad's! Megan got the point and shut up—for then.

I'll have to admit the gym was filled with excitement. Kids were running around with hammers putting up booths. The place was full of crepe paper, snowflake cut-outs, and all kinds of wintery props.

Frankly, I couldn't tell what most of the stuff was

going to become. One booth looked pretty much like the next.

We finally got Oswald to stand upright. Personally, I thought the wooden props behind him didn't look too sturdy. Well, what do I know?

Our committee also built and decorated the ticket booth. The seventh-grade boys did the building, and I stapled dark blue material over the frame. Megan stuck on the snowflakes. Several guys watched her. But not Matthew.

When one committee got the P. A. system hooked up, somebody started playing a record. And then the whole place went crazy! Until Mr. Schneider got things under control.

Mostly, the girls were talking about who would be "queen." Naturally, I couldn't let on I knew about Heidi!

Finally, we were done, and it was time to leave. I hate to admit it, but I was so tired I was glad when Megan's father dropped me off at home. I'll have no trouble getting to sleep tonight. That's for sure!

Chapter 6

Horse Sense – and Dollars

Lord, it's me, Jennifer.

Having my whole family file into Twin Pines Stables to look at Snap was not my idea. And my brothers weren't all that thrilled either.

"Do we have to go?" Pete asked. "The guys are going sledding."

"Yeah," Justin complained.

"Getting a horse is like getting a new member of the family," Dad explained.

"A brother or a sister?" Justin wanted to know.

Everyone looked at me. "Sort of a brother," I said.

"All right," said Justin.

"You can be excused when we get home," Mom said. "Chris is coming to discuss what we're getting into."

If Chris is coming, I'll stay," said Pete.

"Dad!" I whined. In our family, whining isn't permitted. But no one noticed.

It was finally decided that after we saw Snap, Dad would drop the boys off at the place where everyone was sledding.

When we assembled in front of Snap's stall, Chris was already there. She opened the door and stood inside. "I won't go into a lot of detail," she said, "but Snap has what's called good *conformation*. That means he has no serious faults and lots of good points."

"He looks good to me," said Mom. Well, naturally, she doesn't know anything about it, but I guess she thought someone ought to say something.

"The stable vet has checked him over regularly, and Snap is in excellent physical condition," Chris continued.

"How old is he?" Justin asked.

"About eight years," Chris said.

"Then I won't be the youngest anymore," Justin said, smiling.

"You won't be the biggest eater either," Chris said. "Snap eats about twenty pounds of food a day!"

Mom groaned. "At least I won't have to cook it!"

Chris continued. "Horses are measured by *hands*. There are four inches in a *hand*. Snap's height, to this point on his back, is fifteen *hands,* which is a good size for Jennifer."

40

I reached in my pocket and touched the carrot. Personally, I think Snap was expecting it. But he stood quietly anyhow.

"One reason I can recommend Snap is that I've watched his behavior during Emily's lessons. He's smart and gentle. He has no bad habits, and his disposition is excellent."

"Sounds better than most people I know," Dad laughed.

"As I told Jennifer, he has a little spirit. But she's done so well with her lessons that I'm almost positive they're well matched." She smiled at my family. "Have I forgotten anything?"

"Just the carrot," I said. I put it into Snap's feed box and gave him a gentle pat.

* * * * *

We took our sandwiches into the family room so we could eat while we talked. I soon learned that if you have to ask what having a horse costs, you probably can't afford it.

"Owning a horse is a lot of responsibility," Chris said. "It isn't like a bowling ball or tennis racquet. Snap will depend on you for everything."

"Well, sure," I said. "But I have to go to school."

"That's why I'm assuming you'll board him at a good stable."

"Like Twin Pines?" I asked.

She smiled. "Right."

"I'll go every day," I said.

"Wait a minute," Mom said. "You don't have Felix to drive you around, you know. That would tie me up every afternoon!"

"As long as Snap's care is arranged for, Jennifer wouldn't have to go every day. But one of the bus routes from her junior high goes right by the stables. She could take that instead of her regular bus."

"A super idea," I said.

"Felix could probably take her home sometimes," Chris offered.

"I could even pick her up on my way home from work," my father said. "At least on the days you can't, Sue."

"How often should I come?" I asked Chris. "Will I have time for other activities?"

"Sure," she said. "Very few people ride every day. Most come two or three times a week, and once over the weekend. We could work out a lesson schedule and some time to practice."

"Don't forget your schoolwork," Dad said. "I have to know your grades aren't slipping."

"Promise," I said.

"You're sure this is what you want?" Dad asked.

"More than anything in the world," I replied. Well, it was dramatic, anyhow!

"OK," Dad got out paper and pencil. "What kind of money are we talking about?"

42

I held my breath while Chris told him. I had no idea what to expect.

"Well," Dad said, "you're sure he's worth it?"

"Maybe even a little more," Chris said.

"I guess it could be worse," Dad smiled.

I was just starting to relax when Chris continued. "The owners will sell you all the tack at half what it cost them. You know, saddle, bridle, halter, grooming equipment." She named another price.

"Oh, boy," Dad said.

"It's a beautiful saddle," Chris said.

"It ought to be," Dad said.

"I checked into the monthly stabling and feeding fee at Twin Pines," Chris said, and named another figure.

"For that I could send him to college," Dad replied. "There's more?"

Chris nodded. "He'll need shoeing every month. And the vet checks him a couple of times a year. With a hack this good, you probably will want insurance."

Dad looked stunned.

"Transportation won't be a problem, unless Jennifer decides to enter shows." Chris was thinking hard. "I guess that's it."

"I could do some baby-sitting," I offered.

"May I make a suggestion?" Chris asked.

"Please do," said my father.

"Emily's parents are willing to lease Snap for a while and let you use the tack. That would give you a chance to try it out before making such a large commitment."

"This isn't a commitment," said Dad. "This is a major investment."

I felt awful. I knew owning a horse would be expensive, but obviously I hadn't thought of everything. However, I absolutely refused to cry! If ever a moment called for maturity, this was it!

Suddenly, Dad smiled at me. "The lease arrangement sounds good to me. How about you, Jennifer?"

"Oh, Dad," I said. "Can we?"

He took out his checkbook, wrote a check, and handed it to Chris. "Here's my earnest money. As soon as the owner draws up a contract, I'll sign it." He wrote, "Lease with option to buy" on a piece of paper and gave that to Chris too.

Mom was smiling too.

"I'm pleased with your decision, Mr. Green," Chris said. "If I've forgotten anything, I'll be glad to answer any questions."

"You've been an excellent agent," Dad told her. "I hope you get a commission."

"I never even thought of that," Chris laughed. "I'm excited for Jennifer! And it will be great to have her at Twin Pines with me!"

"I agree," I said. "For sure." And when I hugged Dad and Mom I realized my cheeks were wet.

Chapter 7

Streak of Happiness

Lord, it's me, Jennifer.

Have You ever noticed how often bad things seem to happen in streaks? Like blowing a quiz, and losing your best pen, and getting a rip in your coat, and then having somebody get cancer. Or even, like my grandpa, die.

No offense, but I've heard that some people react by wondering if there is a God! Probably You've heard them Yourself! Or they question if You really are in control. Like, how could God let everything go wrong? But, personally, I don't blame You. That's when I need You the most. I mean, I *know* I can't handle the hard stuff by myself!

But sometimes lots of *nice* things happen in a streak!

You know, like for me right now. First, I learned how to be friends with a guy. As a matter of fact, I learned it twice—once with Matthew and once with Mack.

Then I learned more about being friends with a girl. Of course, I'm talking about Heidi, the best friend I've ever had! And, as You know, I found out that being cool isn't the only thing in life that counts.

And now my fantasy of having a horse is coming true! Really, Lord, it's almost too much to handle all at once.

What I want to tell You is that I am thankful! It's complicated, You know. Do people forget about You when everything good is happening? Do the same people who say You aren't real in hard times think You're real in the good times? Know what I mean?

Anyhow, Lord, I really want to include You when I'm not having problems. I'm glad You're in on things even when I don't *think* I need You so much. Like now! I'm so happy! Are You smiling too?

* * * * *

I had to call Heidi. "How's Cinderella? Is your dress finished?" I asked.

"You should see it!" she replied. "But, of course, you will see it. Tonight. I still can't believe I'm really queen of the Winter Carnival! Do you think I'll wake up and find it's just a dream?"

"I doubt it," I assured her. "Unless we're both dreaming. Guess what?" I said.

46

"You got a new outfit?"

"Nope."

"Jennifer!" she squealed. "You're getting the horse!"

"Right! Emily's parents just called my dad. They've accepted the offer. I can't believe it!" I told her.

"That is so wonderful," she said. "Have you told your grandmother yet?"

"We'll be calling her tomorrow."

"I want to hear all about it," she said. "But I can't talk long now. Dad is expecting a call."

"What are we wearing tonight?" I asked.

"I hadn't even thought about it," she admitted. "All I could think about was the white dress."

"Naturally," I said. "Do you think kids will dress up?"

"You're asking me?" She laughed. It was kind of funny since Heidi usually asked *me* about clothes!

"Let's look at it this way." I tried to reason it out. "It isn't really a party, so dresses are out. And we wore jeans last night to put up the decorations. That leaves skirts or nice slacks. Sorta like what we'd wear to a basketball game, don't you think?"

"As a friend of mine would say, 'What do I know?'" Heidi laughed. She's started saying it too.

"I'm glad we're going together," I said. "I don't think either Matthew or Mack suspects a thing."

"You'll help me change, won't you?" she asked.

"Naturally. What time?"

"I have to be ready at nine-thirty," she said. "Miss Vanella said I can dress in the teachers' lounge. She'll

47

meet us there a little after nine. She said she always helps the queens."

"How will you get your dress to school?"

"Miss Vanella is going to take it for me. We have to drop it off at her house, naturally," Heidi said. "I have no idea where she lives."

"Check the phone book."

"Got it. Here it is. Gladys Vanella." She read the address. "It's not far away."

"When it's time for you to change, give me a signal," I said. "OK?"

"Shall I ask if you want to go to the rest room with me?"

"I don't know," I said. "You'll think of something when the time comes."

"Jennifer," she said. "I'm kind of scared."

"Don't worry," I said. "You'll knock 'em dead!"

"Huh?"

"Just an expression, Heidi. It means you'll be wonderful. Don't worry about it," I explained. "See you tonight!"

I hung up the phone.

"What's up?" Mom asked from the family room.

"Nothing," I said, as I headed up to my room. "Why did you ask?"

I decided on my blue skirt, with a white blouse and argyle vest. While I was transferring my things into my new navy shoulder bag, I got another phone call. Mom called me and said I could take it in the master bedroom.

"It's Chris," she said. She sounded different.

"Thanks for everything you did!" I said.

"You're welcome. Want to get a hamburger tonight at Reuben's to celebrate? My treat!"

"It's a terrific idea!" I said. "The only trouble is I have other plans. Tonight's our school's Winter Carnival. I'm sorry, Chris."

"That's OK," she said. "It was just an idea."

"How about tomorrow?" I suggested. "Do you think I could try riding Snap tomorrow afternoon?"

"Sure." Chris' voice sounded louder. "Why not!"

"How about two-thirty?"

"Fine."

"Hang on. I'll check with Mom." I went downstairs. "Mom said she'll drive me," I told Chris. "By the way, would you like to come back with me afterwards and go to youth group?"

"Is that at your church?"

"Uh huh. It's all junior-high kids. Mostly the same ones that go to Sunday school and church."

She didn't answer right away. "I don't think so," she said. "I'm not really into religion, you know."

"Once last summer you asked me to tell you about God," I reminded her.

"Did I? I don't remember," she said. "Do you still want to meet me in the afternoon?"

"Of course I do," I told her. "Hey, Chris, I'm not trying to change you or anything. I think you're terrific!"

"Thanks," she said. "See you at two-thirty."

"I can hardly wait," I told her. As I hung up, I realized my voice sounded hollow. But then I remembered the phone upstairs was off the hook.

Chapter 8

Winter Carnival

Lord, it's me, Jennifer.

When Matthew rang the door bell, I was all ready to go. Naturally, we smiled at each other. This time there was no sound of bells in my head. How come, Lord? Well, I suppose people couldn't go through life with bells always ringing.

"Let me help you with that," he said as he took my coat. And this time I managed to get my arms in the sleeves without pawing the air. Much more cool.

"Another basketball game?" Dad came into the foyer.

"Oh, Dad!" I said. "It's the Winter Carnival! You knew that! I'm sure I told you we decided on a winter theme."

"It was Jennifer's idea," Matthew said. "For some strange reason it hadn't been done before!"

"It's funny that our real snowstorm nearly called it off," I said.

"Lucky it stopped snowing when it did," Matthew agreed.

"Very lucky," Dad said. "What time will you be home?"

"Is eleven-thirty all right?" Matthew asked. "Dad's picking us up."

"Fine," Dad agreed. "Have fun!"

I knew we would. I slipped a little on our front step— not on purpose. Well, naturally, Matthew gave me his arm to hang onto. And then, just as he finished helping me into the car, he slipped himself—and fell!

"Are you OK?" I asked.

He grinned as he dusted off the back of his jacket and pants. "Nothing hurt but my dignity!"

"Which doesn't bruise easily," Mack said, from the front seat. "Hi, Jennifer!"

"I hope Oswald doesn't fall," Matthew said, as we waited for Mack to come out with Heidi.

Soon they appeared. I noticed that she didn't hold his arm. Neither of them slipped anyhow.

Mr. Harrington drove us to school. I could tell it was him because of his hat. But he's gotten so good at not saying anything that it was sort of like having Felix! As soon as Matthew can drive, we won't need a parent!

"Isn't it funny how different the school seems at

night!" Heidi said. She hadn't talked much. Just smiled. We tried not to look right at each other because we were afraid we'd give away the secret!

The four of us stuck together. We stopped at each locker to hang up our coats. Then we headed to where the action was—the gym.

"I can't believe it!" I said. "It's really beautiful, isn't it?" Instead of the bright ceiling lights, millions of little Christmas lights had been strung around most of the room.

The sound committee was playing "old favorite" winter music, some of it Christmas carols. And the mob of kids had responded by keeping their voices down. Well, naturally, they were laughing and talking, but no one yelled.

"We need a system," Matthew said. And we all laughed. It sounded like Matthew, all right.

"For what?" his brother asked.

"For going to the booths. Let's start at the first one on the left and take them in order."

"We don't have tickets," I said. Instead of having the kids at the booths collect money, everything was to be paid for by tickets. They could be purchased at the booth I helped decorate.

"Good point," Matthew said. He took my hand and we headed to the center of the gym. Heidi and Mack stuck with us.

The four of us each bought a book of tickets. Heidi and I paid for our own.

Then we went back to the first booth, which happened to be the Snowball Throw. We had to throw white balls (not really snow, of course!) to try to knock down bowling pins. Spotlights were focused on the pins so we could see them.

"Heidi, you go first," Mack suggested. After missing entirely on the first ball, she got two pins down. Which wasn't bad at all. We all cheered.

Throwing isn't my best thing. At least not small balls. I was relieved to get one pin down at the end. Everybody cheered. I laughed. It wasn't a big deal.

"My turn," said Mack. We watched with fascination as he got every single one. Even other kids cheered.

When Matthew took his place, I could hardly stand to watch. *Please help him, Lord!* Matthew is the only non-jock in the Harrington family, something I found out only recently. But I've gone through this with my brother, Pete, all his life. I held my breath.

He threw hard. But not accurately. He threw hard again. And missed. Suddenly, he looked right at me. I smiled. He grinned. Relaxing, he lobbed the ball and knocked down two pins at once. And, for good measure, he lucked out on the last pin too.

As we all cheered, Mack thumped him on the back. "Attaboy! Way to go!"

"It was a miracle," he told me, as we headed to the next booth. "Would you have ditched me if I had missed them all?" He smiled at me.

I smiled back. "What do you think?" I said. And then

I thought I heard sleigh bells. Of course, it could have been the music.

In one booth, we got our picture taken—all four together. We sat in a row in an old-fashioned sleigh with a blanket over our laps. Then somebody took a Polaroid picture. They told us to wait until we were sure it turned out. Well, it was so sensational that each of us wanted one, so they ended up taking three more shots. I put mine and Matthew's into my purse so they wouldn't get bent. And Heidi kept hers and Mack's.

As we walked around, I noticed that not many girls were there with guys. Sometimes a group of guys would stop to talk to a group of girls. I didn't notice anyone there all alone.

"Anybody hungry?" Matthew asked.

Naturally, we all were. At one booth, they had ice cream cones with coconut on top. Although they cost three tickets each, we decided to go for it.

Not only were they delicious, but we got to sit in a special place with park benches! I'm sure the point was to keep the food from getting all over the gym, but I personally thought the result was sort of romantic.

The only trouble is that I hate getting sticky. And eating an ice cream cone that drips really makes me nervous. So I ate it real fast.

"You must have been starved," Matthew said.

"Not exactly," I said. "But if I told you my reason for eating so fast, you'd probably laugh at me."

"Try me," he said.

He didn't laugh. When he took his last bite, he reached for my hand. "Doesn't feel a bit sticky," he reported.

Well, Lord, there was this mirror "ice-skating pond" with candles "floating" on it. It was in the middle of the park benches. And the tape was playing "White Christmas." And I felt like I was in a movie.

And then Heidi and Mack were standing by our bench. "Jennifer," she said, "I was wondering if you would like to come with me?"

"A good idea," I said, giving her a *knowing* look. One the guys would certainly interpret it as a visit to the rest room. "How about if we meet you in a little while down at the cakewalk?"

"Winner shares all!" Matthew said.

"See you later," said Mack.

I smiled at Heidi and looked at my watch. It was five after nine.

Chapter 9

Long Live the King – and Queen

Lord, it's me, Jennifer.

Since I've never been in a teachers' lounge before, I didn't know what to expect. But it really isn't any big deal. As You probably know.

When we got there, it was locked. Heidi knocked softly, and Miss Vanella opened the door.

"And how is our beautiful queen?" she smiled.

"Nervous," Heidi said.

"Your dress is lovely!" It was waiting on a hanger.

Well, for sure, she was right! Mrs. Stoltzfus had turned that material into a vision of loveliness. But would it fit?

I stood there. "I'm Jennifer Green," I told the teacher. "I'm Heidi's friend. She asked me to help."

"Hi, Jennifer. Mr. Hoppert's been telling me about you," she said. "I teach ninth-grade English."

I didn't know what to say. As they say, I really have a way with words!

Heidi was washing her hands. Miss Vanella finished unbuttoning the white dress and handed Heidi the slip. "Here, Jennifer," she smiled. "You can use this hanger for Heidi's regular clothes."

Well, Heidi wasn't saying anything. She put on the slip and changed her shoes. The white ones looked like something left over from several years ago. I hoped they wouldn't show.

"Here we go," Miss Vanella said softly. The dress, which buttoned up the back, fit perfectly.

"Wow!" I said. To be honest, it couldn't have been better! The style was excellent. Somehow it managed to avoid looking like either Snow White or a bridal gown. It was appropriate and cool all at the same time!

"I brought pearls," Heidi said. "Do I need them?"

"Let's decide later," Miss Vanella said. She dusted Heidi's nose with powder. "I think under that spotlight you'll need a little blush," she said. "Hold still for a minute." Next she touched Heidi's eyelids with blue.

"My hairbrush is in my purse, Jennifer," Heidi said. I handed it to her, and she brushed her soft curls.

"May I try it?" Miss Vanella asked. She performed some more magic with Heidi's hair and then said, "Now for the crown!"

It was in a blue box. It looked kind of cheap just lying

there. But when she put it on Heidi's head, the crown could have belonged to Lady Di herself!

"I'm glad I got the contacts," Heidi laughed. She was loosening up. "At least I won't fall!"

"What about the pearls, Jennifer?" Miss Vanella asked. She held them up.

"I'm no expert," I admitted. That's for sure! "But don't they detract from the crown?"

Heidi and I both looked at Miss Vanella. She agreed. "OK if I add a touch of perfume?"

Heidi nodded. "Do you know who the king is?"

"It's a secret," the teacher laughed. "I don't know myself. One of the men is helping him right now."

"Do you think I'd better go?" I asked. "Matthew and Mack will be wondering where we are. Unless you still need me."

"I'll stay with Heidi," Miss Vanella said. "It's my happy responsibility to see that the queen appears at just the right time."

I went over and kissed my friend's cheek. "Heidi, you're the most beautiful queen in the whole world." I said.

"Thanks, Jennifer. Meet me when it's over!"

"I will," I promised. "We all will!"

The funny thing is that Matthew and Mack didn't even realize I had been gone a long time. They were really into the cakewalk. I waved to get their attention. Mack waved back. And then it was over, and a plump girl I've never seen before got the cake. It figured.

"I'm disappointed," Matthew said. "That chocolate looked so good. Hey, Jennifer, where's Heidi?"

"She'll be along," I said. "We ran into a teacher who needed something. And you know how Heidi is about helping." They knew.

But then there was a drum roll. And the president of the student council was standing on the platform next to Oswald, the styrofoam snowman. Someone had put up Christmas trees with tiny white lights. The tape was playing "Winter Wonderland." And I thought I couldn't stand the suspense.

"Heidi's going to miss this," Matthew said.

"She's coming," I promised.

All the spotlights in the booths were turned off, leaving the gym a galaxy of twinkling stars. Well, naturally, they were really Christmas-tree lights, but the effect was similar.

Everybody stopped and looked at the platform.

"You didn't come to hear me give a speech," said the student council president. "Although I'm tempted!" he laughed. I could hear giggles. The word was out that he planned to go out for debate in high school next year.

"This year's King of the Winter Carnival is. . . ."

Everybody waited. Suddenly, a spotlight shone on the platform. "The winner is Harold Boswell! Better known to all of us as 'Dunk'!"

The whole place went up for grabs. Everybody cheered and clapped. And Dunk Boswell stepped into in the spotlight.

"Way to go!" somebody yelled.

"Ready for the big game?" someone else hollered.

Instead of a basketball uniform, Dunk was wearing a light blue tuxedo! Grinning, he unbuttoned his jacket. He pretended to dribble a ball and leap up for a hook shot. Everyone cheered as he rebuttoned the coat.

Gradually the noise died down, and I could hear kids whispering. "And," the student council president said, "here's what we've really been waiting for!" He paused dramatically. "This year's winner for Queen of the Winter Carnival is . . . Heidi Stoltzfus!"

And there she was, standing in the spotlight and looking fantastic!

Heidi stood there smiling just like she always does, and the whole gym went bananas! I mean, there were cheers and clapping and whistles!

Right up there, in front of everybody, Dunk Boswell gave a victory signal, like he does after a basketball game. And then he took Heidi's hand and held it up.

Matthew was trying to tell me something. And Mack was trying to tell us both something. But it was so noisy all we could do was grin at each other and join the applause.

Dunk now had the microphone. "Every victory is sweet," he said. "But some are sweeter than others!" He put his arm around Heidi, and somebody took their picture.

Now Heidi held the microphone. She was as calm as if she'd been a queen all her life. "I don't know what to say," she said. "This is such an honor. Thank you very much." She kept smiling.

The kids loved it. While everyone watched, a crew carried on white "thrones" so Heidi and Dunk could sit down. While "Winter Wonderland" kept playing on the tape, our king and queen took their places. Oswald swayed, but to our relief, the snowman looked down approvingly.

Somebody was taking lots of pictures.

"Did you know?" Matthew asked me, as the brighter lights were being turned on.

I nodded and grinned. "But I couldn't tell anybody," I said. "Heidi's mother made her dress. Doesn't she look beautiful?"

"I can't believe it!" Mack said. And then he laughed because that's usually *my* line. "I thought she had a chance. But it was almost too much to hope for. So often it's the jerks that win!"

Matthew pounded his brother on the back. "How does it feel to be here with the carnival queen?"

Mack laughed and looked up at the platform. "Right now, I think Dunk is better off! Tell me," he grinned, "if I had run for king, do you think I'd have gotten it?"

"I'd have voted for you," his brother said. "How about you, Jennifer?"

I smiled and nodded.

"Well, that's two votes anyhow, Mack," Matthew said. "Who knows about the rest!"

Gradually, after the lights were all on, we edged up to

62

the platform. Dunk was talking and Heidi was listening to him.

"Hey, Dunk," Mack said to his teammate, "you're hogging the ball. My turn!"

"I thought I got to keep her for the evening!" Dunk teased.

"Wrong-o," said Mack.

Heidi stood up. "Please, Sir King, may I be excused? The peasants are at the gate." She smiled at Dunk.

"How could anybody refuse that smile?" Dunk said. "You may go—for now!"

Heidi came over to us. "How'd I do?" she asked.

"Oh Heidi! You were terrific!" I said.

"Congratulations," Matthew added.

"You've always been a queen," Mack told her. Then both of them blushed. Matthew and I laughed.

Miss Vanella took some pictures of Heidi standing alone. "I think," she said, "the ball is almost over. May I help you change?" Naturally, I went along, but there wasn't really much for me to do.

Outside, it was snowing slightly when Mr. Harrington picked us up and took us to Friendly's. For ice cream, naturally. What else? The four of us laughed and acted silly. Heidi and I gave the guys their copies of the picture of us all in the sleigh.

"Oh, I forgot! Did you win at the cakewalk?" Heidi asked. Her costume was in a suitcase. Of her regal splendor, only her blue eyelids and blusher remained. And, of course, her smile!

Later, when Matthew took me to my door, I smiled happily. "Hey, there really is a Santa Claus!" I said.

"Don't you mean there really is a God?" Matthew asked.

"Well, sure," I said. "But He doesn't always let the nice kids win!"

"Every now and then," Matthew said, "He has one who can handle winning!"

"You know," I replied, "I think you're right!"

"Of course," he said, smiling and squeezing my hand.

Chapter 10

Test Ride

Lord, it's me, Jennifer.

I don't know how our Sunday-school superintendent finds out stuff so fast. (How does he?) But Mr. Williams bowed and kissed Heidi's hand when she walked in the door. Heidi blushed.

"May I present her royal highness, Heidi Stoltzfus!" he said with mock dignity.

The kids cheered. But I think the Harrington brothers and I were the only ones who realized what had happened last night. Us and Mr. Williams.

"What happened?" Kelly asked Heidi. All the kids in our class wanted to know.

"Last night was the Winter Carnival at our school,"

she said. "Actually, lots of kids worked on it. In fact, the theme was Jennifer's idea!"

"And Heidi was elected queen," I said, when it looked like she wasn't going to tell them. "It was a real honor! She wore a white dress and everything!"

After things settled down, Mr. Williams reported about his wife. As You know, she has cancer. "Thanks for your prayers," he said. "The treatments are going well. And our faith is being stretched bigger and bigger as we trust God for our family needs."

Matthew's Sunday-school teacher prayed for the Williams', and we all joined in.

"This is the Advent season." Mr. Williams said.

I glanced around. Everyone else seemed to know what that meant. I'd have to fake it and find out later.

Mr. Williams continued. "I decided we'd spend time looking at verses in the Old Testament that predict the details of Jesus' birth."

Aha. *Christmas!* I thought.

"Today," Mr. Williams said, "we'll check out the place where Jesus was born. Which was . . . ?"

"Bethlehem," everybody said.

"How do you know? Give me a specific verse."

Matthew read from his Bible. "'So Joseph also went up from the town of Nazareth in Galilee to Judea, to Bethlehem the town of David, because he belonged to the house and line of David.'"

"Where did you find that, Matthew?"

"Sorry," Matthew said. "From Luke 2:4."

Kelly raised her hand. "I'm reading from Matthew 2:1 'After Jesus was born in Bethlehem in Judea, during the time of King Herod, Magi from the east came to Jerusalem.'"

"Now," said Mr. Williams, "did you know that Jesus' birthplace was predicted ahead of time?"

Well, Lord, I didn't, that's for sure.

"Look up Micah 5:2," Mr. Williams said.

I knew I'd never find it! I never even heard of Micah before. But suddenly, as I flipped through the pages of my Bible, there it was! I raised my hand, and Mr. Williams nodded.

"'But you, Bethlehem Ephrathah, though you are small among the clans of Judah, out of you will come for me one who will be ruler over Israel.'"

When I finished reading, Mr. Williams told us that what I read had been written hundreds of years before the verses in the New Testament. Lord, that's really awesome!

Later, during church, I tried hard to listen. I loved singing the carols. But concentrating was a problem. As You know. Sorry!

* * * * *

Mom dropped me off at Twin Pines exactly at two-thirty, and I waved as I went in. Since I didn't see Chris, I went over to Snap's stall.

He knew me right away! In fact, he was standing there

waiting for me. I reached into my pocket for the carrot, then watched him eat it.

Without other people around, I got a real good look at the horse. He was dark brown, almost black in places. But there was a white spot on his forehead.

I patted him while I introduced myself. "I'm Jennifer," I told him. "Jennifer Green, that is. And I've been wanting a horse for more than a year."

His ears twitched. I knew he was listening!

"I think you are beautiful, you know." I couldn't stand it any longer. I climbed into the stall with him, and reached for the bridle.

"You're going to be one of my best friends," I told him. "I can tell." He watched me. And he stood still as I reached up to hug him. Hugging a horse isn't easy when you're standing on the ground. But I think he got the idea. I put my face next to him and closed my eyes. "I can't believe it," I said.

"But it's true!" Chris stood watching us. She was smiling, but her eyes looked red.

"Hi," I said, smiling back. "Are you OK?"

"Fine," said Chris. "Why don't you saddle up?"

"What a beautiful saddle!" I said. I was careful to place it properly before I fastened it. "Here you are," I told Snap, as I raised his front legs so he wouldn't get pinched. When I inserted two fingers between Snap and the girth, I grinned at Chris. "How's that for perfect?"

"You may need to adjust the length of the stirrups," Chris said. "Emily was shorter than you."

I measured against my arm. "What do you think?"

"It should reach your armpit," Chris said. "Why don't you let it down?"

Snap moved and I jumped. "Easy, boy," I said. "I've never done this before."

Chris opened the door, and I walked out. Although I had done this often with Rocky since summer, I felt different now. I hoped I could handle him well.

We had to go right past Rocky. I felt disloyal and guilty. I couldn't bear to look.

"All right," Chris said, "Let's see you mount!"

I swung up and settled gently into the saddle. It felt as if it had been made for me. I took up the reins with both hands. Chris had taught me well. Surely Snap would realize that I was no beginner! But why did I feel so nervous?

Chris must have realized that I was waiting for her to tell me what to do. "OK," she said, "walk to the right."

Suddenly, I felt as if I had been riding all my life. I applied pressure with both legs, straightened my back, and loosened the reigns a little. Snap moved gracefully. "Wonderful!" I whispered. His ears were alert.

As we moved together into a trot, I could tell I was grinning from ear to ear. But I didn't look at Chris. I looked straight ahead and tried to act cool. It was no use!

"Let's see him canter!" Chris said. I watched for the next corner and felt Snap's response to my leg motion.

"Beautiful, Snap!" I said. I had a little trouble bringing him back into a trot because I leaned forward. But it wasn't a big deal. I walked back toward Chris and stopped directly in front of her.

"Super!" Chris said. "Both of you! I've never seen a better first ride!"

"I can't believe it," I said. "You're a super teacher, Chris!"

"You have a super horse!" Chris replied. "Emily never could handle him that well!"

I never felt happier. I patted Snap and said dumb things to him.

"Why don't you practice?" Chris suggested. "I'm going to ride awhile myself." Although this wasn't really a lesson, I was surprised.

My earlier nervousness had disappeared. I was happy for the chance to practice downward transitions. All that means is slowing down! Naturally, we had to go faster before we could slow down. I was getting hot!

When Chris returned, she paid no attention to Snap and me. I had never seen anyone ride like she was doing. The tension in her face relaxed as she seemed to forget everything that had been bothering her.

"I love you, Hoagie," she told him. "More than anybody in the whole world!" Mostly, I couldn't hear what she said. And I didn't even want to. A person has a right to some privacy!

"Time to stop?" Chris asked, looking at her watch.

"I can't believe how fast the time went," I said.

We both spent a lot of time grooming our horses and talking to them. At least I talked to Snap. Maybe it was just as well that their stalls weren't together!

70

"I'm feeling like a new person," Chris said, as we sat waiting for our rides home.

"What was wrong?" I asked, although I was pretty sure I knew.

"The usual," Chris said. "Mom kept us up almost all night with her drinking. And on Friday she was really terrific. Hey," she added, "I'm starting to sound like my dad."

"I'm still going to youth group," I said. "Want to reconsider and come along?"

"Nope," she said. "I'm glad you enjoy it. But I just don't think I'd fit in."

"The kids are neat," I said.

"Not this time, Jennifer," Chris said.

Just then I saw Mom's car. "Will you be here tomorrow?" I asked.

"Naturally," she said. "Will you?"

"Are you kidding?" I laughed. "See you then!"

Chapter 11

Chris
Confides in Me

Lord, it's me, Jennifer.

Mondays are usually kind of dippy, but today was stranger than most. For one thing, we hadn't had school on Friday because of the snow. And, naturally, lots of things can happen over a three-day weekend!

"Hi, Jennifer!" Stephanie greeted me like a long lost friend. And Lindsay even smiled again. "Hear you're buying Emily's horse!"

"How did you know?"

The girls smiled mysteriously. "Are you planning to change stables?" Lindsay asked. "There's room where we board our horses, you know."

"I'm sticking with Twin Pines," I said.

"Think about it," Stephanie said. "You could ride with us."

Well, as You know, I couldn't tell her how I really felt!

Matthew and Mack waved to me. They stood on a bank of snow with some of the guys. I waved back.

The bus was late. The roads still are packed with snow, although now there's sand on the hills.

When Heidi got on, the kids cheered. Both guys and girls congratulated her as she made her way back to her seat beside me.

"You're a star!" I told her.

"What's that?"

I couldn't believe it. "You know. A hit. Famous. A ten. Number one."

Heidi just laughed. Then she changed the subject. "You said you'd tell me more about your horse," she reminded me.

Well, I didn't need lots of encouragement. "He is incredible!" I said. "Fifteen hands high, which is perfect for me. It's like we were meant for each other."

"Maybe you were," Heidi said.

"Mom is calling the school today to arrange for me to take the bus route out to Twin Pines after school. Then she won't have to take me all the time."

"Will you ride every day?" Heidi asked.

"Not every day. But lots," I said.

"Maybe sometime I can come to watch," she said.

"Any time!"

At lunch we had just started talking about Mrs. Williams when Stephanie and Lindsay came up to our table.

"Mind if we join you?" Stephanie asked, smiling.

The nerve! I thought. *Just because Heidi won the contest!*

"We'd love to have you," Heidi said. "Wouldn't we, Jennifer?"

"Sure," I said. As You know, it was a lie!

* * * * *

When I entered the stable, Snap was watching for me. All day long in school I had daydreamed about seeing him again. I thought the last bell would never ring!

To be honest, my horse looks better than yesterday. Better, even, than I remembered him. I decided I'd borrow my brother Justin's camera to take his picture.

"Want your picture taken?" I asked. "Want to be a star?"

To be honest, I'll have to admit to You that it is hard for me to tell if he knows what I'm saying when we're in the stall. Probably he's getting used to my voice. When I'm riding him, we have signals!

I hated to leave Snap even long enough to put on my riding clothes. But I had no choice.

"You got here fast," Chris said.

"The bus idea was terrific!" I told her. "Of course, the kids wondered who I was and where I was going."

"Want me to give you a lesson today?" Chris asked.

75

"What do you think?"

"How about just getting more used to riding him," Chris suggested. "Maybe a lesson Wednesday?"

"Great," I said. "Then will you ride now too?"

"Might as well." She smiled. "Riding is my getaway with a friend," she explained. "Hoagie always listens and never gives me grief," she explained. "I'll meet you!"

Two other girls were in the ring. Although they said "Hi," they were involved with their own horses. Riding isn't a very social hobby.

Well, I can't tell You how much more confident I felt today! Of course, maybe Snap felt more used to me too. Whatever is happening, we're a super team!

Riding indoors involves manege exercises. That is like riding on a huge rectangular game board with markers on the corners and in the middle of the sides. Instead of being called Boardwalk or Marvin Gardens, the markers are called *A, K, E, H, C, M, B and F.*

The two other girls turned out to be beginners, so Chris and I had a hard time keeping four feet behind the horses in front. That's the rule!

But Snap obeys instantly. And I guess the discipline didn't really hurt either of us.

The time went incredibly fast. I looked at my watch. "I'm going back," I told Chris. "I want plenty of time to groom Snap."

Chris smiled. "That shows you really love him," she said. "I hate it when people just ride and don't give the horse any attention!"

"Good Boy," I told Snap, as I tied him up. The first step in grooming is to pick out his feet to remove the dirt, but they didn't really need it. So mostly I brushed. Last summer Chris had taught me to groom Rocky. Grooming is more fun when it's your own horse!

"I can hardly stand it," I told Chris later. "I have an orthodontist appointment after school tomorrow. I'd rather be here!"

"I know," Chris said. "Would you like me to look in on Snap and make sure he's OK?"

"Oh, Chris," I said. "That would be wonderful!"

"Mom said I can invite you to come for dinner again," Chris said.

"No kidding," I said.

"Dad wants to meet you too," she told me. "I didn't realize how much I've been talking about you!"

As You know, the only time I've eaten at McKennas' house was last summer. They live in a mansion that nearly knocked my socks off. On the other hand, Mr. McKenna didn't even come home. And Chris and her mother quarreled.

That's when I found out that Mrs. McKenna drinks. The funny thing was that I wouldn't have even known it if Chris hadn't told me! That's because I don't have experience. I don't think Chris tells many people about her mom.

"How about coming home with me on Wednesday, after your lesson? My father promised he'd be home that night," Chris told me.

"I'll check," I said. "Oh, no! I have a huge social studies test Thursday! I promised Dad I'd keep my grades up!"

"Then I'll have to call you about another date," Chris said. "Of course, you realize that any plans are subject to how Mom is feeling!"

"It must be hard," I said.

"Not really," Chris said carefully. "I've just gotten so I don't count on anything anymore. Only Hoagie."

"You've got Nellie and Felix," I reminded her. He's their chauffeur, and she's their cook. They are married to each other. And very nice, in my opinion.

"Nope," she said. "Not since I realized that they might leave if Mom gets too bad."

"You don't know that," I said.

"True, but if I don't count on them, I know I won't get hurt." She was very serious.

"OK if I change the subject?" I smiled.

She smiled. "Of course."

"Does a horse always have to have the same name?"

"Don't you like Snap's name?" she asked. She always catches on before I explain things.

"I'm not sure," I admitted. "I think I'd feel more like he's mine if I could name him myself."

"Do you have a name in mind?" she asked.

I shook my head. "Not really."

"Well, a horse's real name will always stay the same," she explained.

"What's Snap's real name?" I was surprised.

"I don't know," she said. "Every horse is registered under some name that's on his papers. But they usually aren't called by their registered names."

"Then *Snap* is just what Emily called him?" I asked.

"Probably. Think you can do better?"

"I don't know," I said. "But I'm going to think about it. If that's permitted," I said.

Chris grinned. "It's permitted," she said.

I saw Mom's car. "See you Wednesday," I said.

"Right!" she smiled. I think Chris is glad to have me there no matter what she says about Hoagie!

"You look very happy," Mom said, as I tossed my tote into the back and slid in beside her.

"I do?" I asked. "Why do you suppose that is?" I glanced over at her. She was grinning too.

Chapter 12

I Am Invited

Lord, it's me, Jennifer.

After dinner, I went right to my room to study. Well, naturally, I loaded the dishwasher first. All through our meal, all I just wanted to think about was having my own horse!

"Tell us about the Winter Carnival," Mom said. "Were the kids surprised about Heidi?"

"Keever was!" Justin said. Keever is Heidi's younger brother, and in the same grade as Justin.

"So were the Harringtons," Pete reported. His classmate is Mike.

I just let them hog the conversation. Saturday night seemed a long time ago. To me, at least. I pictured Snap eating his carrot. And to think I nearly forgot to give it to him!

"But how about the kids at school?" Mom asked again.

It took me a minute to remember her point. Which was Heidi and the Winter Carnival. "Well," I said, "of course, I don't see the kids in seventh or ninth grades. But the eighth graders are happy. Always before, a ninth grader got it. So Heidi's kind of a star! Even the kids who used to ignore her talk to her now."

"Grandma sure was happy, wasn't she?" Justin said. "How come Jennifer got to talk so long?"

"I also had to tell her all about Snap," I explained.

"So, how is Snap?" Dad asked.

Well, that's all it took to get me started. Talk about hogging the conversation! I was still at it when Justin cleared the table for dessert.

"Watch out!" Justin said. "Matthew might get jealous."

"Of a horse?" I scoffed. "No way!"

"Announcement!" Mom said. "Before you leave the table, I want to remind everybody that the youth-group spaghetti supper is going to be at our house this Saturday night. No mess in the family room!"

"Is the basement off limits too?" Pete asked, looking at me.

"I'll let you know," I said.

"There's a high-school basketball game anyhow."

"No, there isn't," I said.

It was just our basic family mealtime.

Afterwards, Dad stopped next to the dishwasher and smiled at me. "I've never seen you so happy," he said.

I smiled back. "It's even better than I thought," I told him. "Snap and I were meant for each other! I can't wait for you to see me ride him!"

"I'm looking forward to it too," he said.

"By the way," I announced, "I'm not taking any phone calls! I'll be in my room studying." I thought my parents would faint.

At first, hitting the books was tough. But I have no choice. If my grades go down, no horse! You know Dad! He's always been very big on us doing our best in school.

I started out by writing another theme for Mr. Hoppert's class. The assignment was to tell how to do something. I wrote a funny explanation of how to get off a horse! (One way is *falling!)*

Next, I read my social studies. We are studying "Our Neighbors". Well, actually it really doesn't mean *neighbors!* It's just the author's way of describing countries not very far away from the United States.

I'm especially turned on by pictures of palm trees. Probably because they remind me of Florida and being warm! But our test will cover stuff like natural resources. As usual.

When I closed my social studies book and looked at my watch, it was after nine. I put on my robe and went downstairs. Mom and Dad were watching television.

"Any calls?" I asked.

Mom waited a minute for a commercial to come on. "Mack Harrington wants you to call him about chairs for the youth-group party," she said. "And Chris wants you to call her. Get lots done?" she asked.

"Lots," I said. I headed for the study. There I could sit down while I talked.

"It's Jennifer," I said when Mrs. Harrington answered. "Mack asked me to call him back about youth group."

"Hi, Jennifer!" Mack said. "You turning into a brown nose, or something?" He laughed.

"Not really," I said. "But I have to keep my grades up. It's part of my agreement. Did you know I'm leasing my own horse?"

"Doesn't everybody?" he teased. "You've probably even told the mailman!"

"I have not!" I said. "I don't even know the mailman!"

"Then that's why you haven't told him," he laughed. "I forgot to write down how many folding chairs we'll need for the party."

We reviewed the table and chair situation. "You'll bring them, right?"

"Right," he agreed. "I think that does it! It's going to be a great party."

"I hope so," I said. We're in charge, and I feel very responsible. "See you tomorrow."

When I called Chris, she answered the phone herself.

"McKennas' residence," she said.

"It's me, Jennifer."

84

"I thought it might be!" she said. "My father will be home for dinner tomorrow night. Any chance you could come here after your orthodontist appointment?"

I thought a minute. I could study in Dr. Crawford's office while I was waiting. "I guess I can, but I'll have to check with Mom."

"Felix said he'll be happy to pick you up and bring you home. Dad's coming back from Wilmington with a customer."

Mom wasn't too thrilled about my going out on a school night.

"I think she's lonely and needs encouragement," I said. "I'm the only one she talks to about her mom's drinking problem. She never has kids over."

"You can't stay late," Mom said.

"I won't," I said. "Felix will bring me home. Is nine OK?"

Mom nodded, and I rushed back to the phone. "Sorry to be so long," I said. "I can come!"

"Super!" Chris said. We worked out all the details, including my having to be home by nine o'clock. Then I headed up to my room.

Laying out my clothes for tomorrow was tricky. I wanted to look cool at McKennas' house, but I wouldn't have time to change after school or the orthodontist. I decided on a skirt, with boots, blouse, and vest. At the last minute I added a tie. I hoped nobody would laugh.

Frankly, Lord, I'm kind of scared. Can you make it so Chris' mom won't be drunk? And, as You know, I've never even met Mr. McKenna. Last time he didn't show up. Please don't let that happen again!

And, by the way, can You help me find a new name for Snap? It's no big deal. I'll stick with Snap if I have to. What do You think? Would he get all confused?

Anyhow, thank You that I'm so happy. You can tell, can't You?

Chapter 13

Another Dinner at McKennas'

Lord, it's me, Jennifer.

I felt stupid sitting alone in the back seat with Felix driving. We talked enough for me to find out that he had already taken Chris home. But I honestly couldn't think of anything to say. I guess chauffeurs aren't big on starting conversations either.

So I sat in the dark remembering what it was like last summer when I had dinner at McKennas'. Because Chris taught riding at Twin Pines and cleaned out her horse's stable, I had decided she was poor!

I remembered Mom's and my surprise when we saw the McKenna mansion! I felt like I was entering a movie or something. It had been hard to act cool.

The other main thing I remembered was how beautiful Mrs. McKenna was. Her white hair was perfectly styled and groomed. And her long, flowing red dress showed up against the silky, blue sofa. Also I remembered her very sweet voice, when she said, "Christine."

But I really was confused when Chris quarreled with her mother! How was I supposed to know Mrs. McKenna had been drinking? It wasn't obvious like the drinking on television.

"Well, here we are," I said, as Felix turned into the lane. *Brilliant!* I thought. But it was all I could think of to say.

Felix opened the door for me, and I got out. I felt dumb carrying my school books, but I didn't know what else to do with them.

"Hi, Jennifer!" Chris was waiting at the door. I've never seen her look so happy. Something must be going right!

"Is there some place where I can ditch these books?" I whispered.

She grinned and took them to a table in the huge entry hall. They looked stupid next to the Christmas greens and lighted candles.

"Wow!" The huge, circular staircase was decorated with holly and clusters of fruit. It looked like the cover on one of Mom's magazines. "We don't have our decorations up yet," I said. "Mom's going to wait until after the youth-group party."

"When's that?" Chris asked.

"Saturday," I replied. We were walking toward the tremendous, white-carpeted living room. But once I saw the lighted Christmas tree, I lost my thoughts of anything else. "Wow," I said again.

I mean, we're talking gigantic! In any normal-sized room, a hole would have to be cut in the ceiling. As Chris and I stepped down into the living room, the tree looked even bigger.

"Hello!" It had to be Mr. McKenna. When he first stood up, I didn't realize how tall he was. But by the time we stood next to him, I could see he is taller than my father. He has a boyish smile. And laughing eyes. "You must be Jennifer Green."

I felt comfortable immediately. I smiled back. "Correct," I said. "And you must be Mr. McKenna."

"How do you do?" He bowed with fake formality.

"Hello, Jennifer." Mrs. McKenna remembered me!

"Hi!" I said. "You sure look beautiful." I think I said that to her last time. But it was still the truth. And, once again, I had said the right thing.

She was pleased. This time her flowing "bathrobe" was black velvet. She wore pearl earrings and necklace. I was glad I hadn't worn something dumb like jeans!

As for Chris, she hadn't said anything. But her smile tonight was genuine. Happiness is having both parents home and acting normal.

"I'll bet you're hungry," Mr. McKenna said. "How about a cigar?"

Well, I didn't know what to say. Naturally, I've never

even considered smoking anything at all. Much less a cigar!

Mr. McKenna has this hearty, warm laugh. "That's what we call our favorite hors d'oeuvres," he said, turning toward a table. *Some help that was!* I thought. *I don't even know what an hor d'oeuvre is!*

Mrs. McKenna went first, and I watched her so I'd know what to do. She served herself several items from a large platter. One looked like rolled up sausage stuffed with something white. It had to be the cigar!

I figured there'd be more to eat than this, so I didn't take much. Chris' dad poured something in a cup and handed it to me. Suddenly, I felt very nervous. But it was just hot spiced cider like Mom makes.

It wasn't easy talking and eating and drinking at the same time, especially since I had to concentrate on not spilling anything on the white carpet! But I made it.

"Dinner is served," Nellie announced. She wore a black and white uniform the same as last time.

I didn't know where to put my plate, but Nellie took it. "Hi, Jennifer!" she whispered. I grinned.

Well, it was one awesome dinner, I want You to know. I kept thinking I was on TV. Frankly, I've never seen so much silverware. At our house, we get one fork each. I tried to watch Chris, since she knows the ropes.

"I hear you have a new horse," Mr. McKenna said.

That was my cue. "I'm very excited about it," I told them. "I guess Chris probably told you she's the one who worked things out."

"My own favorite mount is a dark bay also," said Mrs. McKenna. "Christine says yours has a star."

I hate to feel stupid. But I had absolutely no idea what she was talking about. I couldn't even fake it.

"The white spot on Snap's face," Chris explained. "It's called a *star*."

"I forgot," I said, taking a deep breath. "Do you ride too?" I asked Mr. McKenna.

"We do a little fox hunting," he said.

"Oh," I said. Which was kind of twinky. But you do what you can!

They asked me about my parents and brothers. And our move to Philadelphia from Illinois. I talked so much I had a hard time finishing my dinner. They had to wait for me so Nellie could take away our plates.

During dessert (homemade apple pie!), Mr. McKenna told funny stories about when he was a boy. He lived on a farm! Everybody laughed. Even Chris' mother, some of the time. But the happiest of all was Chris.

"I'm sure you want some time to yourselves," Mrs. McKenna said sweetly after dessert. "If you'll excuse us, we're going into the den."

"Sure, Mother," Chris said.

Chris led the way up to her room. It is still like I remembered it—full of ribbons from horse shows. She closed the door quietly. "Thanks for coming," Chris said. "It was super!"

"Hey," I said, "I think that's what I'm supposed to say!"

"This is the most fun my family has had in ages!" Chris told me. "Maybe things are going to change."

"I don't know how this will hit you," I said. "But I did pray about tonight."

It didn't hit her. "Dad and Mother did it for me!" Chris said. "I told them I was going to run away. But they must love me after all!"

"Of course they do," I said. "Anybody can see that. And you're a very special person, Chris McKenna."

"You always make me feel good," she said. "You and Hoagie."

"What's Hoagie's real name?" I asked.

"Son of Callahan" Chris said. "Cool, huh? And I bet I know what you're going to ask next." We both laughed. "For your information, Snap's registered name is *Andromeda*."

"You've got to be kidding!"

"Nope," Chris laughed. "Maybe you could go with 'Andy' for short."

"No wonder Emily called him Snap," I said. "I can't even remember that! Do you have some paper so I can write it down?" She did.

I looked again at her ribbons. "I really will be able to enter horse shows now, right?"

"Right!" Chris said. "At least by spring. I've been wondering if you'd like to start learning to jump?"

I couldn't believe it! "Are you sure?"

"How about tomorrow? You're ready for a lesson, if you want one."

"You really are serious, aren't you?"

"I always am," she said. And that's pretty much how it is with Chris.

I hugged her. I was so happy, I just had to.

There was a knock on the door. It was Nellie, reminding us about the time. She said Felix would be waiting with the car in the circular drive.

"I'll ride with you!" Chris said. "OK?"

"Great!"

She didn't even have to ask her parents. She took her coat out when she got mine from the closet. "Don't forget your books," she reminded me.

We chattered all the way back to my house. The trip goes much faster when you have a friend along.

"Oh, no!" I said.

"What's wrong?" Chris asked.

"I forgot to thank your parents!" If she knew, my mom would be horrified.

"It's OK. I'll tell them for you." Chris was so happy. I'll never forget the look on her face when we said good-bye.

Naturally, I looked pretty happy myself. As You probably noticed.

Chapter 14

What Happened to Chris

Lord, it's me, Jennifer.

I took the piece of paper and the carrot out of my pocket. "Andromeda," I said to Snap. All he did was look at the carrot. Which figures! No horse in his right mind would answer to a name like that! A name I can't even remember! I'm surprised he didn't laugh!

"Andy?" I tried. He reached for the carrot. I gave up and put it into his feed box. Like it or not, I guess we're stuck with "Snap."

After changing into my pants and boots, I saddled my horse and was ready to ride. I kept expecting to hear Chris' greeting. Two other girls said "Hello," but I don't know their names yet.

"Well, Boy," I said to Snap, "we might as well get started." He followed me out of the stall.

After some warm-up rounds, I settled into practicing the posting trot. Since Snap's gaits are smooth and easy, I need to practice posting with his motion. That sort of means not leaning too far forward and moving with the horse's moves.

"Good, Boy!" I said. "Let's try it once more." All this has a point. I need to be comfortable with posting before I can learn to jump.

Finally, we both got tired. I looked at my watch. Chris still wasn't there.

"Did Chris McKenna call or leave a message?" I asked a man who works at Twin Pines.

"Not that I know of," he replied.

"Could you check?"

He didn't seem too thrilled. "Didn't call," he said when he returned. "And she's supposed to let me know if she wants me to take care of Hoagie." He acted bothered by the extra work.

Personally, I was bothered about Chris. I hoped nothing had happened to her. It wasn't like her not to show up.

I rode some more, but my heart just wasn't in it. I decided to spend extra time grooming Snap.

"What could have happened?" I asked him. Well, naturally, he couldn't tell me.

"She was so happy last night. And she knew how excited I was about starting to jump." I brushed harder.

Brushed and polished. Brushed and polished.

"Maybe I could try to call her!" But the man in charge said the phone was just for emergencies. "I don't know if this is an emergency or not," I told Snap. "What do you think?" Well, at least he listened.

I was waiting for Dad when he drove up. "I'm worried," I said. "Chris didn't come."

"Isn't it as much fun by yourself?" Dad asked.

"You don't understand," I told him. "She's always been there before! I was supposed to have a lesson." I wondered if I should mention what Chris said about running away. I decided not to.

"Maybe she called you at home," Dad said.

Well, she hadn't called. At least not while anybody was there. So I tried her number. No one answered.

I tried again after supper. The telephone rang four times. Then someone answered! "McKenna residence." It was Nellie's voice.

"Nellie," I said, "this is Jennifer. Jennifer Green. May I please speak to Chris?"

There was a pause. "She can't come to the phone," she said. "I'm sorry."

"Nellie," I said, "is something wrong?"

"I'll give her your message, Miss. Good-bye." She hung up.

I felt frustrated. And worried, Lord! It finally dawned on me that at least Chris was safe at home! Please help her, Lord!

With my social studies test tomorrow, I really had to

study. I was glad I hadn't let it go until the last minute. But I was having trouble keeping the different countries straight.

"May I use your globe?" I asked Dad. That helped a lot. Some of the places weren't much farther from the United States than we are from Illinois!

"I have a message for you," Mom told me, when I went downstairs for a break. "From Chris."

"Why didn't you call me?" I asked.

"She didn't call. Felix told me to tell you Chris will meet you at Twin Pines after school tomorrow."

"That's it?" I asked.

"That's it," Mom said.

* * * * *

Chris was there, dressed to ride, when I arrived. Hoagie was all saddled. "Jennifer, I'll talk to you later," she said. "I need to ride first." She mounted Hoagie. She didn't smile once.

I watched her go. I had no choice. But just seeing Chris made me feel better.

It didn't look like I was going to learn to jump this week. But seeing Snap was excellent. "I aced the test," I told him. He seemed glad. We feel comfortable together now, sort of like Matthew and me.

Later, Chris and I sat in the corner of an empty stall. "It's all my fault," Chris said.

"What's all your fault?" I asked.

98

"I shouldn't have ridden home with you. Mom was drunk when I got home. And Dad walked out and didn't come home. And Mom blamed me all night long." She took a deep breath before she continued.

"And when Felix and Nellie took my side, Mom fired them. And then Dad came home and was mad that I hadn't gone to school." By now she was crying. I didn't know Chris could cry.

"So I just took off on one of our horses. I just rode and rode and rode. And then the police found me," she sobbed. "I had to go back."

"I don't know what to say, Chris." Tears were running down my cheeks too.

"Don't say anything," she told me. "Please! I shouldn't have told you. It's my problem, nobody else's. You've got to promise me you won't tell anyone." She looked frightened.

"I promise," I said. There was no way I could get out of it, Lord. Promising, I mean. "Are Felix and Nellie gone?"

"Dad bribed them to stay. He said if a word of this gets out, he'll be ruined. I shouldn't have told you."

Chris stopped crying. We both sat there quietly in the dark. I could hear someone walking around in the stable.

"Want a carrot?" I said. "I forgot to give it to Snap."

"Sounds good," she replied. "Let's share it."

So we munched in the dark.

"Sorry I missed your lesson," she said.

"Don't be stupid," I told her. "That's the last thing in

the world you should have to worry about. Besides, I practiced posting with Snap's motion. He's much smoother than Rocky was."

"That was a good idea," she said.

All the time, I was racking my brain trying to think of something happy for Chris to look forward to. "Chris," I said, suddenly, "can you come to my house Saturday night? Our youth group is having a spaghetti supper."

She didn't answer right away. "It's just a party?"

"Uh huh. Sort of. You could meet my friends from church."

She didn't say anything. "At least I'd have a good excuse to be away from home," she said, finally.

"So, does that mean you'll come?"

"I guess so." A car honked, and we both got up.

"Seven o'clock," I told her.

"Jeans?"

"Sure," I said. "Jeans will be fine."

Lord, did You make that idea pop into my head? And did You encourage her to come? More than anything in the world, I want Chris to know about You. Is that how You feel also?

Chapter 15

Let the Party Begin

Lord, it's me, Jennifer.

Having a party, especially an Italian dinner, isn't a *piece of cake*. (Sorry, but I couldn't resist that!) Even though we had committees and stuff, there was lots to do at the end.

After school on Friday, Mom took Leslie Ann and me shopping for the food. Fortunately, Mom is very organized, or we'd never have made it! She had lists for everything.

In the evening, while we were stirring huge kettles of tomato sauce in the kitchen, Mack and several other guys arrived with tables and chairs from the church. "Where do they go?" he asked.

Since our family room is huge, we were able to fit in the three long banquet tables with room to spare.

"Mom!" I called. "Want to check the tables?"

She looked hot. Something red had spilled on her apron. But she was smiling. "Perfect!" she said. I think she enjoys getting ready for a party.

"Anything else we can do?" Mack asked. As You know, he's cochairman. With me, that is.

"Are you planning to have a fire?" Mom asked us.

Mack grinned at me. "I'm all for it," he said. I guess he was remembering the night of our first social committee meeting, when we got the idea for this party.

I also remembered. After the others had gone home, Mack and I sat and talked by the firelight. That was when I first realized I liked both Matthew *and* Mack!

"Well?" Mom smiled at us. "Are you planning to have a fire, Jennifer?"

"Sure, Mom," I said, "why not?"

By now, only one person had to stir the sauce, so the rest of us set the tables. One reason we decided on an Italian dinner was that Mom already had three matching, long, red-checked tablecloths. We put two candles on each table. I thought it looked great.

After the preparations were finished, I thanked Mom again. "It's going to be a great party," I said. "I'm so excited that Chris is coming."

The next morning, Mom asked if we'd be using the living room. "It looks so bare. I think we need some Christmas decorations around." she said.

"We'll be having a mixer in here," I told her. "You know, a game to get people talking and moving around."

"Punch would be nice, wouldn't it?" Mom asked. "During the mixer? I can easily make some."

"Thanks, Mom" I said, "that would be nice."

Mom decorated the room with a few angels, a needle-point cut-out that says *JOY* (which my aunt made), and our beautiful manger scene. "We'll do the rest of the decorating next week," she said.

In the afternoon, Heidi called to see what I was wearing. "I was thinking of my long skirt," she said.

"Would you consider jeans?" I asked.

"To a Christmas party? You've got to be kidding!"

Well, naturally I wasn't kidding, but she had a right to wear whatever she wanted to.

Chris would be wearing jeans. So that's what I'd be wearing also. Otherwise, she'd feel awful. That's for sure. After all, what are friends for?

* * * * *

My brother Pete had spent all afternoon taping Christmas music. And Dad had mounted a wreath on the front door. The spotlights were a nice touch. Mom helped me light the candles on all the tables in the family room. It looked cosy and romantic, even without the fire lighted.

I wore a white blouse with my jeans. Whenever I felt tempted to feel sorry for myself, I thought about what Chris had gone through this week. As the doorbell rang,

Pete started the tape. "Deck the Halls With Boughs of Holly!"

The first arrivals were a whole group of kids who live kind of near Kelly. Suddenly, the house was alive with noise and laughter.

Heidi arrived alone, wearing a beautiful velvet skirt and a new sweater. She carried a box full of cards and pins. After the kids hung up their coats and entered the living room, she pinned a card on the back of each person.

I kept watching for Chris.

"May I get you some punch?" Matthew asked me.

"Thanks. That sounds good."

"Care to join the party?" he teased. Then he turned around so I could see his back. "Am I something from the first Christmas?"

I laughed. His card said *reindeer.* "No," I said.

He turned me around. "Hey, where's your card?"

"I'll have to get one from Heidi," I said. "But I hate to leave the door. Chris is coming. You know, my friend from Twin Pines stables."

"I'll watch the door for you," Matthew offered.

"Thanks," I said. As I threaded my way through the kids, I noticed cards that said *wiseman* and *stocking* and *inn* and *angel.*

"Here you go, Jennifer," Heidi said. I could feel her sticking a pin through the card and my blouse.

"Am I a modern Christmas custom?" I asked her.

"Ask someone else," Heidi laughed. "I'm only responsible for the pinning! I don't give clues too!"

I walked up to a ninth-grade guy. "Am I from the first Christmas?" I asked.

"Yes," he told me. "Am I?" He turned around.

I started to laugh. "Yes," I said. I couldn't stop laughing. His card said *Mary!*

I remembered Matthew, waiting at the door. "Maybe Chris forgot," he said.

"I hope she's all right," I said.

Just then the doorbell rang. The kids nearby stopped talking and watched as I opened the door. It was Chris. But naturally, except for me, no one knew her. So no one said anything to her.

"Hi, Chris!" I was so glad to see her.

"Sorry I'm late," she apologized.

"No problem," I told her. "We're just getting started." I took out a hanger for her coat.

Matthew thought this was the right time to meet her. "I'm Matthew Harrington. Would you like to come with me to get some punch?" He is so cool.

Chris glanced at me. She looked kind of nervous. I smiled. She looked back at Matthew. "Thank you," she said. "I'd like that."

I watched them go into the crowded living room just as the tape started playing, "It Came Upon the Midnight Clear." I couldn't believe it. She was wearing a beautiful blue quilted skirt!

The point of the mixer was to find out what was written on the card on your back. You could ask one person a question with a *yes* or *no* answer. Everybody was running around asking questions, turning to show people their cards, and laughing.

I decided to try. I could hardly even see Chris and Matthew anyway. "Am I a woman?" I asked Kelly.

She looked at my back. "No," she said. When I offered to answer a question for her, she said she already knew who she was. It figured.

"Am I a man?" I asked Mack Harrington.

"No way!" he said.

I could feel my face getting hot. "I mean my card," I explained. He just laughed.

"Am I alive?" I asked. "I mean, was I alive?"

A seventh-grade girl said no, not exactly.

Well, I really was getting into the game by then. But it took me a while to find out I was the *star!*

Suddenly, I remembered Chris. She was standing near the bookcase pretending to look for a book. As a master at faking it myself, I can spot it easily in others!

"Hey," I said, "I didn't mean to leave you alone. What happened to Matthew?"

"Everybody's playing the game," Chris said.

"Did you find out who you are?" I asked.

"I don't even know what questions to ask," she said.

"Let me see your card." Chris turned around. On her back it said *shepherd*.

"I'll give you a clue," I told her. "It's a character from the first Christmas."

"What's the first Christmas?" she asked.

"Oh, my goodness," I said. "You don't know about when Jesus was born, do you?"

"No. Should I?"

"Well," I said, "it's a story in the Bible."

"You said this was a party!" she told me.

"It is," I assured her. "You're a *shepherd*. Does that mean anything to you?" It didn't. "Well," I said, "I don't have time to tell you now. Just stick close to me and everything will be OK."

But then Mack came up and took Chris' arm. "Come with me, Shepherd. I'm Mack Harrington, and I'm a shepherd too. We're all going to sit together." He guided Chris over to where the shepherds were gathering.

I watched over the flock as they entered the family room. Then, feeling as if I had abandoned my friend, I found a place at the next table. For what it's worth, I sat between the *manger* and *Rudolph*.

Chapter 16

Birthday Party

Lord, it's me, Jennifer.

For the first time tonight I just realized that having a party is a *responsibility.* It's not just making sure there's stuff to eat (my idea), or that the house is clean (Mom's).

Well, as You've probably noticed, I've mostly been concerned with whether *I'm* going to look good, and whether *I'm* going to have a good time. But tonight I didn't have time to think about either one. I was too busy wondering if *Chris* was enjoying herself.

Mostly, I couldn't tell. Since I haven't had much experience giving parties, I couldn't decide if it was better to stick with her or not. I still don't know. What do You think?

Frankly, at supper it was so dark I could hardly see Chris at all. But the candles were romantic. Not that it meant much to me personally. After I asked You to help Chris, I was pretty busy trying to keep the conversation going at my own table.

That's when I suddenly realized that quite a few kids in the youth group aren't all that secure themselves! Getting *the manger* to talk wasn't easy! And the *Angel of the Lord* wouldn't shut up!

When we put on the lights after dessert, everybody groaned. Especially the ninth-grade guys. Which I didn't appreciate, since I wasn't anywhere near Matthew. Or even Mack, for that matter.

After the tables had been cleared, the kids on the committee took them down. Before the next event, I went over to where Chris was standing alone.

"Hi," I said. I smiled.

"Hi, Jennifer."

"How are you doing?"

"OK."

Just then Heidi passed, and I stopped her. "Heidi," I said, "I want you to meet Chris. She's my friend from Twin Pines stable."

Well, as You know, Heidi is just about the friendliest, nicest girl I've ever known. She smiled and said, "Hi, Chris. I'm Heidi Stoltzfus."

"Hi, Heidi," Chris said.

And then there was this incredible silence, while nobody said a word!

110

"What school do you go to, Chris?"

"Dayspring Academy," she said.

"Oh." Honestly, Heidi said *oh!* "Is there a girl there named Amanda Springfield?"

"I don't think so," Chris said. "Maybe she goes to Episcopal."

"Maybe she does."

More silence.

I tried to help things along. "Chris is the one who's taught me all I know about horses," I explained. "She's a wonderful teacher."

"Jennifer's a good student," Chris said.

More silence. I was trying to remember how people break the sound barrier and get to know each other!

Then the next part of the evening began, but that didn't help much either. There were skits about stuff that happened in youth group. Naturally, these were hilarious—to the kids who had been there.

But it couldn't have been much fun for Chris. Although she sat with some of the girls, nobody really said much to her. I don't think anyone was leaving her out on purpose. Still, I felt very disappointed.

Every time I looked at Chris, I remembered how awful I felt when I first moved to Philadelphia and didn't know anybody. Is that how she was feeling?

Mack went over to the fireplace and asked, "Anybody got a match?" In our crowd, that line is always good for a chuckle. See, no one smokes, naturally. Well, You probably figured it out Yourself.

I stood up and handed him some matches from my jeans pocket. "Just happen to have these," I said.

"Perfect hostess!" Mack said. And I got a mild round of applause. I hammed it up a little by pretending to calm down the audience.

As the kindling caught hold, everyone moved around and sat on the floor in front of the fireplace. Matthew joined me and whispered, "How's the *star?*" Frankly, at the time, all I could think of was *where was Chris?*

Ernie, the guitar player, started us singing some camp songs. By now everybody (except Chris, of course!) knows "Peanut Sitting on a Railroad Track." Then we learned a new one that involved jumping up and sitting down. I relaxed as I caught sight of Chris, laughing with an eighth-grade guy.

I must say, it was a beautiful fire! When the logs caught hold, somebody turned off the lights, and we started singing Christmas carols. I kind of thought about Chris and wondered if she knew them. But not too much.

Mostly I felt relaxed and very, very happy! I stopped worrying about Chris and gave myself permission to enjoy the evening! That was OK with You, wasn't it?

With some encouragement from the kids, Ernie sang a solo for us. When I realized it was partly about the star, I listened to every word:

There's a song in the air!
  There's a star in the sky!

There's a mother's deep prayer,
   And a baby's low cry!
And the star rains its fire while the beautiful sing,
For the manger of Bethlehem cradles a King!

In the light of that star
   Lie the ages impearled,
And that song from afar
   Has swept over the world.
Every heart is aflame, and the beautiful sing,
In the homes of the nations that Jesus is King!

All of a sudden I knew it is true. You are King! Yet You left Heaven to come to earth as a tiny baby. Was it hard? Did You mind? You really loved us, didn't You? Well, naturally, You still do!

Then I realized Matthew was talking to me. "What did you say?" I asked. Believe it or not, I had forgotten all about him! You know, this is the first time Christmas has affected me so deeply!

"I said having you be *the star* was special, wasn't it, Jennifer?"

"It's really an honor," I said, seriously. "To light the way to Jesus, I mean."

One thing I like a lot about Matthew is that he doesn't destroy a time like that by making a joke! "The star will always remind me of this Christmas," he said.

"Me too!"

Well, everybody joined Ernie in singing "Silent Night."

It was not romantic. It was beautiful and holy.

Afterwards, so many kids were crowded near the door that I really didn't have much chance to talk to Chris. When Felix arrived to get Chris, he wasn't wearing his chauffeur's hat. So he looked pretty much like the other kids' fathers.

Chris was smiling. "Thanks," she told me. "I'll call you."

I smiled back. "If you don't, I'll call you," I teased.

The Harringtons were the last to leave. By then my parents had come on the scene. It figured.

"It was a terrific party!" Matthew said.

"We were good cochairmen, weren't we?" Mack said to me.

"You bet! And we had a great committee."

"And excellent hospitality, thanks to you, Mrs. Green." Mack shook Mom's hand.

After the guys left, I hugged my parents, Mom, then Dad. "Thanks!" I said. "This really feels like a home now."

"A house needs some happy memories," Mom said. "That takes time."

Upstairs, I couldn't get Christmas out of my mind. Thanks, Lord, for coming to Your birthday party!

Chapter 17

Shepherds and Other Problems

Lord, it's me, Jennifer.

In Sunday school today, Mr. Williams told us that the Old Testament plainly taught that Jesus would be born to an unmarried girl!

First we looked up Isaiah 7:14. Heidi got called on to stand up and read: "'Therefore the Lord himself will give you a sign: The virgin will be with child and will give birth to a son, and will call him Immanuel.'"

Then we all turned in our Bibles to Matthew 1:18 to read how it came true. I found out that *Immanuel* means "God with us!"

Mr. Williams read us the part about how Mary found out she was going to be Jesus' mother. I put a marker in my Bible so I could read it again in Luke 1:26-38.

Now I get the point about how You're the Son of God. Joseph wasn't Your father! Mr. Williams says it was a miracle. I agree!

Frankly, I'm very impressed with Mary! Sure, she had a few questions! Who wouldn't? But she must have loved You a lot to be so obedient! Wasn't she ever embarrassed? I guess the honor was more important.

In the afternoon, my family went to see the Christmas display at Longwood Gardens. It felt strange to walk inside the building from the snowy grounds and see green grass!

No offense. It was beautiful. But I think I would have enjoyed it more with somebody like Matthew. Instead of my family, that is. Pete and Justin acted immature. And Mom walked too slow.

In school, we're heading toward exams. But I'm not very nervous. The more I study, the less nervous I am! And, because of getting my horse, I've been hitting the books hard. Dad doesn't fool around. Bad grades, and *pow!*

I've been going to Twin Pines almost every afternoon. Snap even watches for me! It's true. And I'm beginning to feel as if I've been riding him forever. It's called *confidence.*

On Thursday, after I had practiced fifteen minutes, Chris put a rail on the ground. I noticed it right away, but I acted cool. It is hard to act cool when you know deep inside that you're going to learn to jump!

"Keep me in your line of sight!" Chris said. That means I'm supposed to look at her, not anything else—even Snap. Of course, I've learned to do everything by *feel* right from the beginning.

Chris stood in front of the rail. We may be good friends the rest of the time, but during a lesson she is in charge. I do exactly what she tells me.

"Around the ring at a slow trot in jumping position," Chris said. "Three point contact." I obeyed.

"OK, Jennifer. As you approach the rail, move your hands halfway up Snap's crest. Use the mane to steady yourself. The weight of your upper body is on your hands and Snap's neck."

I tried it. Snap didn't really jump at all. He just trotted over the rail. I felt disappointed.

"Your weight should go into your heels—not the stirrups," Chris said. "Try it again."

The next time Snap made a little hopping jump! I was so excited, I blew my cool.

"Over here, Jennifer," Chris said. I stopped next to her, expecting her to bawl me out. Instead, she just grinned. "Neat, huh?"

"I love it," I admitted.

"As you post with the motion, the horse will thrust you forward and upward. *Wait for the horse!* Snap will do the jumping, not you!"

"Shall I try again?" I asked.

"You got it," Chris smiled. "And again, and again, and again, and again."

So, while Chris watched, I kept practicing. Just when I thought I had it, I'd blow it. But, on the whole, I was doing all right.

I couldn't believe it when it was time to stop. But then, I never can. Believe that my time is gone, that is. Riding makes time go faster than anything I've ever done.

"OK if we talk while you groom Snap?" Chris asked.

"Naturally," I said.

She sat in a corner. "Tell me about the shepherds," she said.

"They're part of the Christmas story in the Bible," I said. Since I didn't have a Bible with me, I had to sort of wing it. Hope You didn't mind.

"So?"

"They were just watching their sheep one night, as usual. They happened to be in a field near Bethlehem. That's the name of a city. All of a sudden, an angel showed up, and they were scared to death."

"How did they know it was an angel? Wings?"

"I don't know. Maybe because he just appeared in the sky, and there was a bright light," I said. "Well, anyhow, the angel told them not to be scared because he had good news for everybody."

"Which was?"

"In Bethlehem, the city I mentioned, a baby had just been born. Well, the baby was really Christ, the Lord. See, everybody was waiting for God to send a Savior."

"What's a Savior?"

"I'll tell you later. Anyhow, the angel told the shep-

118

herds if they wanted to see for themselves, they could go into town, where they'd find the baby in a manger."

Chris stopped me. "You mean a manger like in a barn?"

"Right," I said. "Then, a whole group of angels came to keep the first one company. They all praised God together."

"Right there in the field?" Chris asked.

"Yes," I said. "So, being the curious types, they all decided to go and see the baby."

"The angels?"

"No. They disappeared. I forgot to tell you that part. The shepherds. Probably the night was shot anyhow. Who could sleep? So they went to see Jesus."

"Who's Jesus?"

"He's really God," I told her. "But He got sent to earth as a baby so we could see what God's like."

Chris was silent. So was I. Between the riding and the brushing and the talking, I was exhausted. Finally, she asked, "Jennifer, can you keep a secret?"

"Sure," I said. I'm getting to be an expert!

"I'm going to a meeting tonight," she said.

I just brushed and waited. Then I stopped and looked at her. She looked scared.

"What meeting?" I asked.

"Promise you won't tell?"

"Promise."

"It's called Ala-teen. It's for kids whose parents have drinking problems," she said. "They meet at a hospital.

Felix is going to drive me over after dinner."

I sat down beside her. "How'd you hear about it?" I asked.

"One of my teachers told me. I don't know how she found out. Maybe because I missed school. At first I wasn't going to go, but then I decided there was nothing to lose. Except for my pride," she added. "Plus Dad would probably kill me, if he ever found out."

"Who's in charge of the meeting?"

"It's part of A.A. Have you heard of Alcoholics Anonymous?"

"I think so, but I've never thought much about it," I admitted. "Is it like a secret club?"

"I think so. Nobody tells that you come."

"Why are you telling me?" I asked.

"Because I know I can trust you," Chris said. "And," she added, "because you're my only friend."

"You *can* trust me," I said. "I hope the meeting's really helpful. Will you let me know?"

"Uh huh."

My dad's car honked. I looked at Chris. I wanted desperately to say something loving and helpful and encouraging and kind. But I couldn't think of anything. As the car honked again, I smiled. "See ya," I said.

Lord, there's only so much a friend like me can do. As You know. I'm really glad she's getting interested in You! At least, shepherds are a start! Right?

Chapter 18

Following Yonder Star

Lord, it's me, Jennifer.

This morning in Sunday school, Mr. Williams asked the junior-high department, "How many Wise-men were there?"

I raised my hand quickly. "Three," I announced. I might not have gone to Sunday school all my life, but I sure knew that one. Well, I was wrong!

"Let's check it out," Mr. Williams said. When we looked in Matthew chapter 2, we discovered that the Bible doesn't tell how many. Did the song writer just make it up? Or when people started having Christmas pageants, could they only come up with three robes?

Well, as You can see, here was the star again! By now,

we were all expecting that there'd be a clue about it in the Old Testament. Sure enough, Numbers 24:17 says, "A star will come out of Jacob."

"The Wise-men were expecting the star," Mr. Williams told us. "And they followed it thousands of miles."

"How long did it take them?" Heidi asked.

"No one knows exactly," Mr. Williams said. "But it might have taken as long as two years. You'll notice that by the time the Wise-men arrived, in Matthew 2:11, Jesus wasn't in the manger." He read: "'The star they had seen in the east went ahead of them until it stopped over the place where the child was. When they saw the star, they were overjoyed. On coming to the house, they saw the child with his mother Mary, and they bowed down and worshiped him.'"

They were in a house! But Lord, how come the pageants and manger scenes always have the shepherds and Wise-men there together? I suppose because it's hard to cover up to two years in one scene! Right?

Here I thought I already knew all about the first Christmas! The point is, it really means more to me this year. After all, it's Your arrival on earth! You really did live here, didn't You? Incredible!

*   *   *   *   *

I spent so much time at the stables riding Snap, that I hardly thought about buying Christmas presents!

"Want to go to the mall tomorrow after school?" I

asked Heidi. "I haven't started shopping!"

"I'll help you," she offered.

Shopping is hard when you don't have much time or money. If you start early enough, you can make gifts. People usually appreciate homemade things even if they aren't useful or even particularly attractive. They'll say things like, "You really spent all that time making that for *me?*" They may not even know what it is!

Well, clearly, this was not to be that kind of Christmas. I had to use my brains, not my hands. Which can be a lot harder!

Without Heidi, I would have given up. "OK," she said. "Let's start with your mother."

I couldn't think of anything inexpensive. That's a nicer word than *cheap*. Mom has several years' supply of cologne. That's what Justin always gets her. Same with kitchen gadgets from Pete.

"How about books?" Heidi asked. "Does she read?"

Well, naturally, Mom reads. She reads a lot. We went to two bookstores, but I hadn't the faintest idea what to pick out. However, I did see several books I'd like for myself.

"How about a gift certificate?" Heidi suggested. "She could pick out whatever she wanted." We went back to the department store. But gift certificates started at $10.00.

"Heidi, you're a genius!" I said suddenly. "I have an idea. I'll even treat you to frozen yogurt while I tell you about it!"

* * * * *

When I got home, I started to work on my idea for gifts. At first I planned to put them in envelopes, but then I realized people might think they were getting money and be disappointed. So I put them in boxes I got from Heidi's mom. Then I wrapped them and scattered them among the gifts under our tree.

On Christmas Eve, I got cold feet. Not really, but You know what I mean. I got this terrible feeling that my idea was dumb and everybody would laugh or think I was cheap. But it was too late!

On Christmas morning, Justin got to be Santa. Personally, I think he's the smallest Santa I've ever seen in my life, but he tried hard. He handed out some of his own gifts first.

"Hey," I said, as I opened my first gift, which just happened to be from him, "what a lovely scarf. And it's just the right color!"

"Mom helped me," Santa admitted. I thanked him, but decided to omit any kissing.

Obviously, Mom hadn't helped him with her own gift. You guessed it! Another bottle of cheap cologne. However, Mom did act thrilled. I think it's part of motherhood training. Before you can have a child, you should pass "Basic Gift Appreciation."

The first person to get one of my own gifts was Pete. The suspense was killing me. He pulled out a card and read it out loud,

         "'Merry Christmas!
   This entitles bearer to two hours of
  my time during Christmas break. Please select
     the activity of your choice.
                 Love, Jennifer.'"

I felt so embarrassed I could hardly look at him. I wished somebody like Dad had gotten his first. He's enthusiastic and would have set a good example.

"Neat!" Pete said. "You know, Jennifer, I've been wanting to try riding your horse. Can I use my card for that?"

"Sure," I said. "I'm not an expert teacher, but I can help you enough that you'll have fun!" As I saw how happy he was, I grinned from ear to ear.

Well, mixed in with the usual gifts, my *time certificates* turned out to be a sensation!

At first, Justin wanted me to clean his room! But then he decided I might throw out something, so he changed his mind. "Will you take me to a junior-high basketball game?" he asked.

Inwardly, I groaned. But a deal's a deal. "Sure," I said, "Name the day!" Santa even hugged me!

When we got to Mom, she said she'd love a day off from cooking! So, I'm in charge of meals next Friday. She even kissed me!

And Dad couldn't make up his mind. "I'm going to think about it," he laughed. "Can't waste such a special offer on just anything!"

Just as we finished the gifts, Dad reminded us that we hadn't opened our stockings!

I felt mine. Sure enough. There's always an orange in the toe. And a new toothbrush. And a bag of chocolate chips! No big deal. But sometimes having things stay the same is sort of comforting, especially after you've moved!

There's usually a small package or two inside each of our stockings. My little box contained pearl earrings. *Pierced earrings!* I squealed and looked at Mom. She nodded. "You have our permission!" I ran over and hugged her first, and then Dad.

"Isn't there something else?" Dad asked me.

It was an envelope. I opened it slowly, half expecting a check. But what I saw was a registration number. When I saw the horse's name, "Andromeda," my eyes filled with tears. I was so shaky that I could hardly keep reading. But the last name on the list of owners said, "Jennifer Andrews Green."

"He's all yours, Jennifer!" Dad said. "All fifteen hands high!"

I was so happy I started jumping around, and laughing, and hugging everybody. My dream had come true!

"What's on the paper, Jennifer?" Pete asked.

"It's Snap's registration paper," Dad explained. "It's like a birth certificate, plus information about his ownership."

Pete looked at it. "How come it says his name is 'Andromeda'?"

126

"Every horse has a formal, registered name," I said. "It always stays the same. I don't even know what 'Andromeda' means, and I'm sure Snap could care less!"

"I know." Pete looked at me.

"Know what?" I asked.

"What 'Andromeda' is."

"Oh yeah?" I said. "What does it mean?"

"Remember Joseph, my friend in Illinois?" Naturally, we did. In Illinois, he was Pete's only friend.

"Well," Pete explained, "one time we got interested in stars. Groups of stars are called *galaxies*. The only *galaxy* close enough for people to see is called the Andromeda Nebula. I think it's sort of like the Milky Way," he told us.

"A candy bar?" Justin wondered.

"No," Pete said. "It's stars!"

I couldn't believe it. Snap even had markings on his face that Chris had called a star! That must have been his name in the beginning.

"From now on, I'm calling my horse Star," I announced.

"If you change his name, will he come?" Pete asked.

"He'll learn," I said, confidently. Otherwise, he won't get his carrot!

"Then 'Star' it is!" Dad said. "A star, fifteen hands high." Everybody laughed.

After our special family breakfast, I called Chris to tell her the news. "Merry Christmas," I said.

She sounded happy. "Same to you!"

"Guess what?" I said.

"I think I already know." She paused. "You now own your own horse."

"How did you know?" I asked.

"I can keep secrets too," she laughed. "By the way, I have a gift coming for you. It's a subscription to a horse-owners' magazine called "Equus.""

"Thanks a million," I said. "I'm sorry I didn't get anything for you."

"Jennifer, having you move here has been the best present of the whole year!" she said.

I felt tears coming again. I took a deep breath. "I've decided to name my horse Star," I told her.

"That's an excellent name," she said. "I suppose you have a good reason."

"Yes," I told her. "As a matter of fact, I have lots of them." I laughed. "And I'll tell you all about it the next time we go riding!"

I felt like I've never been so happy in my whole life. Could You tell?

"Every horse has a formal, registered name," I said. "It always stays the same. I don't even know what 'Andromeda' means, and I'm sure Snap could care less!"

"I know." Pete looked at me.

"Know what?" I asked.

"What 'Andromeda' is."

"Oh yeah?" I said. "What does it mean?"

"Remember Joseph, my friend in Illinois?" Naturally, we did. In Illinois, he was Pete's only friend.

"Well," Pete explained, "one time we got interested in stars. Groups of stars are called *galaxies*. The only *galaxy* close enough for people to see is called the Andromeda Nebula. I think it's sort of like the Milky Way," he told us.

"A candy bar?" Justin wondered.

"No," Pete said. "It's stars!"

I couldn't believe it. Snap even had markings on his face that Chris had called a star! That must have been his name in the beginning.

"From now on, I'm calling my horse Star," I announced.

"If you change his name, will he come?" Pete asked.

"He'll learn," I said, confidently. Otherwise, he won't get his carrot!

"Then 'Star' it is!" Dad said. "A star, fifteen hands high." Everybody laughed.

After our special family breakfast, I called Chris to tell her the news. "Merry Christmas," I said.

She sounded happy. "Same to you!"

"Guess what?" I said.

"I think I already know." She paused. "You now own your own horse."

"How did you know?" I asked.

"I can keep secrets too," she laughed. "By the way, I have a gift coming for you. It's a subscription to a horse-owners' magazine called "Equus.""

"Thanks a million," I said. "I'm sorry I didn't get anything for you."

"Jennifer, having you move here has been the best present of the whole year!" she said.

I felt tears coming again. I took a deep breath. "I've decided to name my horse Star," I told her.

"That's an excellent name," she said. "I suppose you have a good reason."

"Yes," I told her. "As a matter of fact, I have lots of them." I laughed. "And I'll tell you all about it the next time we go riding!"

I felt like I've never been so happy in my whole life. Could You tell?